LITTLE TALES
FROM
AQUAE SULIS

LITTLE TALES
FROM
AQUAE SULIS

LIFE IN ROMAN BATH

BY GERRY MCKEOWN

WITH ILLUSTRATIONS BY ROB GRIEVE

BROWN
DOG
BOOKS

Published under licence by Brown Dog Books and
The Self-Publishing Partnership, 7 Green Park Station,
Bath BA1 1JB

www.selfpublishingpartnership.co.uk

ISBN printed book: 978-1-78545-148-5

Cover design by Kevin Rylands
Internal design by Andrew Easton

Printed and bound by CPI Group (UK) Ltd,
Croydon CR0 4YY

Foreword

'What have the Romans ever done for us?'

Well, apart from the items listed by The People's Front of Judea in 'The Life of Brian' (qv), they gave us the alphabet, our system of numerals, the calendar, judicial system, education system, glass windows, central heating, concrete, public health system, public baths, medicine, hospitals, fire brigades, postal services, civil service, apartment blocks, international trade, etc., etc... However, despite their incredible building and organisational achievements, as well as their legendary leaders, diplomats, writers and scholars, the Romans themselves could be a pretty repulsive bunch at times! For instance, theirs was the only civilisation that killed for pleasure; witness the merciless slaughter of Christians, criminals and animals in the arena, purely to satisfy the bloodlust of the populace. It was with this in mind that these 'Tales' were written. Thus, the stories are about people rather than places or historical events. Some of the names used are the names of real Romans; others have been made up, or have been plucked from a Latin dictionary and as such these latter characters (probably) didn't exist.

The stories were originally inspired by the computer graphic displays in the Roman Baths Museum in Bath, hence the title. The scenes being acted out on the walls of the museum were just asking for dialogue to be added; especially as the Romans did, said, and believed things that are truly bizarre to our 21st century minds. I have tried to put the tales into some sort of chronological order, starting with the Romans' discovery of the Sacred Spring.

Although the stories themselves are fictitious, much of the content has been taken from serious publications (the wording has been slightly altered to avoid breach of copyright!). For example, the story of the Emperor Hadrian at the public baths in Rome (story no. V), is taken from an actual document – *'Historia Augusta – Hadrian part II'*, although I have slightly 'embroidered' it!

The Greek/Roman gods' names, bathing rituals, medicines used, makeup ingredients, foods consumed, birth and funeral rites, marriage ceremonies, school facts and the Legend of Bladud are all taken from actual records.

In the chapter where the Romans and Celts have an exchange of words, each in their own language, ('A Sacred Place' – Chapter III), I have taken appalling liberties with the Welsh language. It seems that the ancient Celtic language in Roman times, and before, is not well understood, so for the purposes of the 'Tales', I have used modern Welsh. I ran my early attempts past some Welsh speakers and can still hear their hoots of derision! However, they kindly gave me a few pointers and I blundered on. The end product is still extremely iffy! My apologies are ongoing!

The stories are peppered with Latin words (in italics),

along with their translations. If readers get nothing more from the Tales than a very basic grounding in Latin, and learn a few little-known facts that I've dredged up, then my living has not been in vain!

In fact, almost all of these 'Tales' are merely vehicles that I have used to illustrate life in Roman Britain.

If, despite my best efforts, the 'Tales' are still sprinkled with inaccuracies, I take comfort from the fact that many of the great Hollywood moguls, such as Samuel Goldwyn, never let historical facts stand in the way of a good story!

A final word before we move on: Despite the many differences between Roman times and our own, it is worth mentioning that some things remain constant throughout the ages. For instance, the following quotation, which is an indictment of the policy of 'change for change's sake', is attributed to the Roman writer, Caius Petronius (27–66AD):

'We trained hard, but it seemed that every time we were beginning to form up into teams, we would be reorganised. I was to learn later in life that we tend to meet any situation by reorganising: and a wonderful method it can be for creating the illusion of progress, while producing confusion, inefficiency and demoralisation.' (Sound familiar?).

The character of Noelius Covardus is partially based on Petronius. Apparently, Petronius was a self-indulgent courtier at the time of the Emperor Nero (54–68AD) and was considered an authority on questions of taste and manners and of the science of luxurious living *(elegantiae arbiter)*. It is believed that he wrote 'Satyricon', a novel which caused quite a scandal at the time. However,

Petronius came to a sticky end when he was accused of treason by Tigellinus, the commander of the Praetorian Guard. The unfortunate bon viveur was arrested, found guilty and obliged to commit suicide!

(My grateful thanks to Mr Stephen Bird, Head of Heritage Services at Bath and North East Somerset Council, for supplying me with the above quotation.)

Introduction to 'Little Tales from Aquae Sulis'

Most of the Tales take place in the Roman Town of *Aquae Sulis*, which we now call Bath, during the reign of the Emperor Hadrian (117AD–138AD). The stories are told, many years after the events, to the pupils (*discipuli*) of a local school (*ludus*), which is run by a wise old schoolmaster (*magister*) by the name of Gaius Lucidus, a man in his 60s, who was born in *Aquae Sulis*, but spent many years in Greece where he learned his schoolmaster's skills. Gaius Lucidus may be fictitious, but the following facts about Roman schooling are not:

• Usually only the children of the well-to-do went to school, and then *almost exclusively boys*!

• Some children of wealthier families were home-schooled by a parent or a home teacher (*Grammaticus*). All teachers were male, by the way.

• Children of all ages, between 7 and 12, were taught in the same classroom in an elementary school by the same schoolmaster.

• Children were taught reading, writing and mathematics. Sometimes they learned to play musical instruments.

• A few of the cleverer ones went on to high school, up to

the age of 15, to learn Greek, philosophy and rhetoric and the sons of very influential people could go on to orator school to learn politics and statesmanship.

• Pupils did not usually sit at desks. They sat on stools or chairs and wrote on a wax tablet (*tabula*) using a bronze or bone pen (*stylus*).

'Clear off, girl! Get back to your pots and pans!'

• The school day started early and finished late in the afternoon, seven days a week! However, pupils had many religious holidays off, as well as summer holidays.

• Naughty or lazy pupils could be beaten by the schoolmaster with a wooden stick!

• Left-handed pupils could also be beaten to encourage them to write with their right hands!

'I plus I is what, boy?'

Anyway, enough of the facts and figures. Now, let's go back almost 2000 years to meet some of the characters who lived (or *might* have lived) in *Aquae Sulis*…

PS. The signpost on the front cover refers to the city of my birth, Glasgow. ('No Mean City'.) The can of lager in the Roman soldier's hand refers to one of my hobbies!

Contents

'Tales' – Some of the Main Characters 15

I. *Fabulam de Bladud*
(The Legend of Bladud) 19

II. *Eruditio de Deos*
Learning about the gods) 25

III. *Locus Sanctus* (A Sacred Place) 30

IV. *Pavor in Aquae Sulis!* (Panic in Bath!) 38

V. *Hadrianus ad Balneis Agrippae*
(Hadrian and the Baths of Agrippa) 48

VI. *Nundinae* (Market day) 54

VII. *Cenerat in villa de Tiberinus*
(Dining at the Tiberinus villa) 61

VIII. *Fons Sancta* (The Sacred Spring) 71

IX. *Mane de Feminas ad Balneis*
(Ladies' Morning at the Baths) 76

X. *Post Meridiem de Hominum ad Balneis*
(Men's Afternoon at the Baths) 84

XI. *Nocte ad Amphitheatrum*
(A Night at the Amphitheatre) 92

XII. *Ut Medico Visitabo* (A Visit to the Doctor) 98

XIII. *'Quis vistis mea furio?'*
('Who stole my clothes?') 104

XIV. *Peregrinus Altaris consecrat*
(Peregrinus Dedicates an Altar) 112

XV.	*Amor et Conjugialis* (Love and Marriage)	118
XVI.	*Partus* (Births)	124
XVII.	*Mors* (Deaths)	130
XVIII.	*Adventus* (Coming-of-Age)	136
XIX.	*Cum Quatuor Temporibus Deversorium* (The Four Seasons Guest House)	141
XX.	*Fabula de Belator* (The story of Belator)	147
Acknowledgments		152

'Tales' – Some of the Main Characters

Aulius Platorius Nepos – Governor of Britannia (122 – 124AD).

Ammonia – Acid-tongued friend of Lady Flavia. Married to centurion, Marcus Aufidius Maximus.

Apulia – A 20 year-old slave of Lady Flavia.

Belator – A 16 year-old slave. The catalyst of the 'Tales'.

Bladud, King – The legendary founder of Bath.

Brucetus – Master stonemason. Father of Sulinus, also a stonemason.

Bilius – Drunken friend of Overseer Gaius Tiberinus and Noelius Covardus.

Cophinus Mucrus ('Copious Mucus') – A 1st century centurion.

Corsog ('Marshy') – A 1st century Druid.

Cantissena – A bad-tempered pilgrim from Eboracum (York).

Devius – A 17 year-old slave. Friend and confidante of Belator.

Ebrius ('Drunkard') – Uncle of Devius. A freedman and stonemason.

Falco, Quintus Pompeius – Governor of Britannia, (118 – 122AD).

Flavia, Lady – Wife of the Overseer, Gaius Tiberinus.

Felix Obesus ('Fat Cat') – Father of Hirsuta, wife of Sulinus.

Gaius Tiberinus – General Overseer of the Baths and Temple Complex.

Gaius Calpurnius Receptus – High Priest of the Complex. Friend of Gaius Tiberinus and husband of Trifosa Calpurnia.

Gaius Suetonius Tranquillius – Secretary to the Emperor Hadrian.

Gaius Lucidus – Local schoolmaster and narrator of the 'Tales'.

Hadrian, (Publius Aelius Triainus Hadrianus Augustus), Emperor of Rome (117–138AD).

Halitus Malus ('Bad Breath') – Dim-witted secretary to Gaius Tiberinus.

Hirsuta Sulina – Wife of stonemason Sulinus.

Ignoramus Maximus (No translation needed!) – A slave dealer.

Lucius Marcius Memor – A Haruspex (augerer) - Friend of Gaius Tiberinus and Gaius Calpurnius Receptus.

Marcus Librerius – An aged scribe at the Baths. Mentor of young Belator.

Machinator – A 1st century engineer.

Maria – a 16 year-old slave and beloved of Belator.

Marcus Aufidius Maximus – A centurion. Husband of Ammonia.

Moribundus ('Dying') – Ancient usher to Gaius Tiberinus and Lady Flavia.

Marcus Medicus – A local doctor.

Medusa Vehemens ('Violent Jellyfish') – Mother of

Hirsuta Sulina.

Marcus Formosus ('Handsome Marcus') – Son of High Priest Gaius Calpurnius Receptus and Trifosa Calpurnia.

Nutricula ('Nurse') – A midwife.

Noelius Covardus (pronounced Cowardus) – Wit and *bon viveur*. Friend of all the important people in Aquae Sulis.

Nausius – A friend of Gaius Tiberinus. He upset Belator on one occasion. (Big mistake!)

Peregrinus – A pilgrim from Trier in Germania. Has a poor grasp of Latin!

Sulis Minerva – The local goddess of the Sacred Spring.

Salmonellus – Cook to Gaius Tiberinus and Lady Flavia.

Sulinus – Son of Brucetus and husband of Hirsuta Sulina.

Trifosa (Delightful!) Calpurnia – An ex-slave and now wife of High Priest, Gaius Calpurnius Receptus.

Vetula Putrida ('Putrid Old Woman'!) – Mother of Lady Flavia and a holy terror!

I.
Fabulam de Bladud
(The Legend of Bladud)

During the reign of the Emperor Septimus Severus and his co-regent, Caracalla (c. 205AD), there was a small school (*ludus*) in the town of Aquae Sulis, in the province of Britannia. The ludus was run by an elderly schoolmaster (*magister*) named Gaius Lucidus. Lucidus was a strict, but fair man and he would reward his pupils (*discipuli*) for their hard work, as well as punish them for sloppy work (or if they tried to write with their left hands!).

One day, the magister told his discipuli that he had a surprise for them. He called for quiet then addressed the class...

'The summer holidays will be with us in three weeks and, as you have all worked so very well and I am very pleased with your progress, I have decided to reward your efforts by telling you some tales of our beautiful city's past. I will tell you a different story every afternoon after schoolwork has been completed.'

There was a buzz of excitement amongst the discipuli at this news. Gaius Lucidus was renowned as a master storyteller.

'Today, for my first Tale, I will relate the story of Prince Bladud. You are all aware of the name Bladud, I'm sure. He was the legendary founder of Aquae Sulis, but you may not be familiar with the details of his legend.

The story begins about a thousand years ago, when the world was a very different place. For a start, our glorious Empire did not exist then. In those days, Greece was the centre of civilisation.

There was once a king of the Britons called Lud Hudibras, who had a son named Bladud. The king wanted his son to have the best possible education in order to prepare him for kingship when the time came, so the young prince was sent on a journey to Athens, the seat of all learning, to be taught by the wise teachers and philosophers of Greece...'

Young Prince Bladud sat slumped in his saddle, his head nodding with tiredness as his horse plodded wearily down the wide road that lead to the city of Athens. He had travelled for many weeks since leaving his home in Britannia, but now his journey was nearing its end. His normally clean-shaven face was covered with stubble, but, as beards were the height of fashion among Greek men, he had decided to remain unshaven.

He was saddle sore and weary to his very bones when at last he reached the outskirts of that legendary city. As he rode into Athens, he gazed around him in awe at the majestic buildings and the magnificently attired Greek citizens. Although he himself was a prince, he felt like a pauper in this place.

Almost humbly, in his best Greek, he asked a passer-by for directions to an address that his father had given him; the home of a distant relative. Bladud was welcomed by his relative who gave him a hearty meal, his first in weeks, then showed him to the room that had been prepared for him.

After a few days' rest, he made his way to the home of an eminent Greek philosopher who had undertaken to be the young prince's tutor.

For the next three years Bladud studied philosophy, rhetoric, mathematics, history and literature.

At last the time came when his tutor decided that the prince had learned as much as he would need to know to rule a small kingdom of Britons; and anyway, Bladud's funds had almost run out and he could no longer afford to pay for his tuition. And so, one day, the young prince bade farewell to his kindly Greek relatives and set off on the long homeward journey.

Such money as he had left soon ran out and for the first time in his life, Bladud was obliged to work for a living. He took many jobs along the way; some dangerous, some dirty; and so almost inevitably, due to the insanitary conditions in which he was obliged to live, he contracted a disease; leprosy.

When he finally arrived on the shores of Britannia and made his way to his father's palace, no-one recognised him. He was filthy, emaciated, dressed in rags and covered in the sores and boils that leprosy inflicted upon unfortunate sufferers. When he was cleaned up and fed it was finally acknowledged that he *was* indeed prince Bladud. However, he was no longer welcome at court due to his hideous disease. He was given a sum of money by the king and then banished from the kingdom. And so, this high-born and well-educated young prince became an outcast, doomed to wander the land; shunned and threatened wherever he went.

However, with some of the money his father had given him, Bladud bought a small herd of pigs from a sympathetic farmer (who kept his distance during the transaction). He hoped that he could barter his pigs at a profit to pay for food and shelter, but found that no-one wished to have anything to do with a leper, even one who owned a fine herd of pigs.

Then the inevitable happened; the pigs contracted the disease from him. The young prince watched helplessly as, day after day, his pigs became sicker and sicker. One day, as this sad company was near the end of its tether, they reached a swampy pond in the middle of a forest where hot water was bubbling up from the ground. The pigs ran into the mud surrounding the swamp and rolled about in it in obvious pleasure. Bladud called to them to come out, but they would not. Hours passed and still the pigs continued to wallow in the hot mud.

In desperation, he collected an armful of acorns, a favourite meal of his pigs, and threw them into the swamp, leaving a trail of acorns back to dry land. The pigs quickly devoured the acorns and finally left the swamp in search of more. As Bladud washed the mud from his pigs he noticed something astonishing; the leprous sores on their skins had vanished! The pigs had been cured of the disease!

Without further hesitation, Bladud waded into the hot mud and immersed himself up to his neck. He lay there hour after hour and when he finally crawled back to dry land he found that his leprosy had been cured also!

He sold his pigs to a local farmer, and then made his way back to his father's court where he was greeted with great rejoicing. He was immediately reinstated as his father's heir.

The young prince vowed that he would return to the place where he had been cured and there he would build a city and a huge temple and dedicate them to the god Apollo, in thanks for his deliverance...

'Did he ever come back?' asked the eager discipuli.

'Remember, this is a legend. It cannot be proved or

disproved' replied Gaius Lucidus. 'However, the story goes on to say that, when he finally became king, Bladud did indeed return to this place and founded a city as he had vowed; our city that we now call Aquae Sulis. The story doesn't end there. The legend says that, because he had had a miraculous cure, Bladud believed that he was a favourite of the gods and that he was invincible, and to prove this he called all the citizens of his new city to the temple of Apollo, where he climbed upon the roof proclaiming to the throng that he could fly!

With that, Bladud launched himself into space, instantly proving that he could not fly and was mortal after all! Despite frantic flapping of his arms the wretched king plummeted to the ground far below. The stunned citizens of the city were obliged to gather up what was left of their king and bury him! That is where the legend of Bladud ends and so does this Tale' concluded Lucidus. 'Class dismissed!'

II.
Eruditio de Deos
(Learning about the gods)

All discipuli in Roman ludi were required to learn the names and functions of the numerous gods and goddesses sacred to the Roman people. However, in the province of Britannia, discipuli in a ludus in the city of Aquae Sulis also learned that many of their deities had earlier Greek equivalents. The magister of the ludus was an elderly man named Gaius Lucidus who, although born in Aquae Sulis, had lived for many years in Athens and so brought much of his learning and wisdom back to the city of his birth...

'Today I am going to talk about the many gods and goddesses who protect the Roman people.' said the magister. 'First of all, do you know who is father of the gods?' he asked. A forest of hands shot up.

'You, Marcus' said Lucidus, pointing to a small boy sitting near the front of the class.

'Magister, the father of the gods is Jupiter' said the lad.

'Indeed he is. Well done!' said Lucidus. 'Does anyone know the name of the goddess of love?' This time not all the hands went up. 'You, Aurelius, can you tell me?'

'I think it is Venus' said the boy.

'It is indeed Venus, Aurelius' said the magister. 'And the god of war? Anyone?' Only a few hands were raised.

'Is it Apollo?' said the youngest discipulus, Lucius.

'No, it is not Apollo' said Lucidus. 'It is Mars. I see I will need to give you a refresher course on the gods. We will continue this lesson tomorrow.'

For the rest of the lesson the magister gave his class some writing exercises, while he sat making copious notes.

The next day Lucidus arrived in class with a bundle of papers under his arm. He distributed these around the discipuli and then sat down on his *cathedra* (schoolmaster chair) and called for quiet.   'Look at the paper before you.' He instructed the discipuli. On each paper was a list of some of the most important Roman gods. The list read as follows:

Jupiter – Zeus (King of the gods and storms; father of Venus)

Venus – Aphrodite (Goddess of love and beauty and gardens)

Mars – Ares (God of war and lover of Venus)

Minerva – Athena (Goddess of wisdom, war, the arts, commerce and industry)

Neptune – Poseidon (God of the seas, earthquakes and horses)

Cupid – Eros (God of love and son of Venus)

Sol – Helios (also known as Sol Invictus, the sun god)

Diana – Artemis (Goddess of the hunt, the moon, virginity and childbirth)

Juno – Hera (Queen of the gods and goddess of matrimony)

Mercury – Hermes (Messenger of the gods and bearer of souls to the underworld)

Pluto – Hades (God of the underworld)

Saturn – Kronos (God of harvest and agriculture; father of Jupiter, Neptune, Juno and Pluto).

Bacchus – Dionysus (God of wine, truth and sensual pleasures)

Terra – Gaea (also known as Terra Mater, goddess of the earth and land)

The discipuli read the list slowly then Marcus, the star pupil, raised his hand. 'Magister, I don't understand. Why have our gods got two names?' he enquired.

'Because, my boy, the second names on that list are those of the equivalent Greek gods or goddesses.'

This caused an uproar!

'How dare the Greeks copy our gods and give them Greek names!' cried the discipuli. 'Who do they think they are? What did the Greeks ever do for us anyway?' they added.

'Actually, it's the other way round' said Lucidus quietly. 'The Greek civilisation is far older than ours, so we copied many of their ideas and adopted many of their gods and goddesses for our own, giving them Roman names. Some we didn't even bother to rename, such as Apollo, god of poetry, music and oracles and Uranus, god of the sky.'

The discipuli muttered amongst themselves, trying to come to terms with this apparent blasphemy. They knew, however, that the magister had studied in Greece and so was very wise and knowledgeable.

'Magister,' said Lucius, the oldest boy in the class. 'Against the god Bacchus' name it says "sensual pleasures". What does that mean?'

'Er, um, I think you should ask your parents when you get home' replied Lucidus, suspecting that the smiling Lucius knew very well what it meant! To change the subject quickly he continued. 'However, we do have many gods of our own who were never part of the Greek pantheon of gods. For example, Janus, the double-faced god of beginnings and endings, and of doors. We also have Cardea, the goddess of hinges and Verminus, the god of cattle worms.'

Seeing the frowns on the faces of his discipuli at the banality of these deities, he pressed on trying to add some dignity to the home-grown gods. 'We also have Cloacina, goddess of the sewers; Laverna, goddess of thieves and vagabonds; Portunes, god of keys and doors; Sterquilinus, god of fertiliser; Terminus, god of boundaries and of course Furrina, goddess of… well, actually nobody really knows!'

Verminus and Portunes

As he summarised in his head the Roman gods he had just mentioned, Lucidus realised that he was only making matters worse and that it was time to bring this lesson to a close!

'Our local goddess, as you know, is Sulis Minerva, a Romano-Celtic deity, who is the guardian of the Sacred Spring here in *Aquae Sulis*' he said. 'One day I will tell you the origins of Sulis Minerva. Have you any final questions before we close today's lesson?' He asked, hoping that the discipuli had had enough for one day.

'Magister,' said Marcus, 'why is our goddess not called Minerva Sulis? Surely Roman names should come first.'

Lucidus sighed. 'That, my boy, is a long story and is best kept for another day. Class dismissed!'

III.
Locus Sanctus
(A Sacred Place)

When the class had settled, Lucidus began his next Tale:
'About a hundred and forty years ago, Roman engineers and
legionaries were mining lead in the Mendip Hills, some 15
miles south west of the area that would become known as
Aquae Sulis, when they learned from their native workers
of a secret spring that was sacred to the local Dobunni tribe.
The Romans decided to visit this place...'

Machinator, the chief engineer and overseer of the lead
mining operations, looked up from the newsletter he had
been reading and addressed the large centurion who was
sprawled on a chair opposite him, coughing into a grubby
piece of linen.

'It says here that the Emperor Vespasian has put a tax
on the use of public toilets in Rome' said the engineer.

'Sounds like he's taxing the pxxx!' chortled the
centurion, whose name was Gaius Cophinus Mucrus,
but who went by the unfortunate nickname of 'Copious
Mucus', on account of his constant spitting and coughing.
The harsh climate in Britannia did not agree with him, or
so he claimed.

Machinator ignored this interruption. 'It says also that when the Emperor was asked why he was imposing such an undignified tax, he replied; "*Pecunia non olet!*" (Money doesn't smell!)'

'Yet some people still get stinking rich!' laughed Cophinus.

At that moment, two of Mucrus' personal bodyguards, Luridus and Nasutus, arrived and crashed to attention in front of the centurion.

'Sir,' said Luridus. 'The Dobunni workmen have asked to be excused work tomorrow morning.'

'What! Whatever for?' Mucrus cried. 'Do they expect to be paid for the time they're not working?'

'Cophinus, we don't pay them all that much anyway' muttered Machinator.

'Um, yes. Well, bring their leaders here and we will find out what this is all about.'

Presently, three Dobunni workers arrived. They gave their names as Optrex, Mordax and Inscritus. They were huge, burly specimens and sported some impressive tattoos.

'Masters,' their leader Optrex began, 'tomorrow is the birthday of our goddess Sul, and we are obliged to make offerings at the Sacred Spring where the goddess dwells.'

'I know of no such spring' said Mucrus.

'It is in a hidden place surrounded by trees, guarded by fierce warriors and protected by the spells of our Druids' said Optrex.

'Your what?' demanded the centurion.

'Druids, master. High priests of the goddess Sul.'

'Perhaps we *could* excuse the Dobunni' suggested Machinator. 'I'm sure your soldiers could continue working on their own for one day while you and I went with the Dobunni to find out more about this goddess and her Sacred Spring, It could be to our advantage and we *do* need to keep the local labourers happy if we are to meet our *plumbum* (lead) production deadlines.'

Mucrus reluctantly agreed with this suggestion and so the matter was settled.

Next morning, the chief engineer, the centurion, their bodyguards and the Dobunni workmen set off for the hidden valley. As they approached the sacred site several hours later, the Romans counted seven hills surrounding the valley.

'Seven hills, just like Rome. This must be a good omen!' enthused Cophinus Mucrus.

At last the party arrived at a clearing surrounded by tall trees. In front of them lay a swamp where hot water steamed and bubbled from it. There was a gravel causeway leading towards the middle of the swamp. The Dobunni halted at a respectful distance from the causeway. 'We can go no further without the permission of the Druids, *Rhufeiniaid*!' said Optrex.

'What did he call us?' said the centurion. 'Sounds like he's calling us ruffians!'

'That is the Celtic name for Romans, or strangers.' Explained Machinator, who had a fair understanding of the local language. At that moment, two figures dressed in long brown robes approached the group. One of them spoke. '*Croeso, Rhufeiniaid, i Gwanwyn Sanctaidd y Sul dduwes!*'

'We're being called bloody ruffians again!' stormed Cophinus Mucrus, reaching for his sword. (Mucrus was not the sharpest *gladius* (sword) in the armoury.)

'Will you never learn?' groaned Machinator. 'The man just said: 'Welcome, Romans, to the Sacred Spring of the goddess Sul!'

The Druid continued in excellent Latin. 'My name is Corsog and this is my colleague, Gwybedyn. To what do we owe the honour of this visit?'

'Our Celtic workers asked to be excused work today so that they might make offerings to your goddess Sul. We would know more of this goddess who commands such devotion' replied Machinator.

'Sul is the goddess of wisdom and protector of holy places. She dwells in our Sacred Spring' said Corsog. 'Each year on this day our tribe gathers to honour the goddess's birthday.'

'We also have a goddess of wisdom, as well as other things. Her name is Minerva. Perhaps you Celts have borrowed our Roman goddess' suggested Machinator.

'Or perhaps it is the other way round' replied the Druid evenly.

'Right! That's it!' yelled Mucrus, reaching for his sword again.

'Oh, for the gods' sakes!' snapped Machinator. 'Look around you! We're outnumbered by about fifty to one!'

He turned to the Druid and said calmly, 'I'm sure you understand that Britannia is now a province of the Roman Empire and if we decide to requisition this spring and dedicate it to Minerva then we will do so.'

Corsog stared at the engineer as the other Celts drew closer to the Druid. The air was charged with menace. 'We would not accept such a sacrilege meekly' said Corsog in a cold voice.

'Are you prepared to fight for it?' snarled Cophinus Mucrus.

'Indeed we are' said the Druid. 'But this is a sacred place and no blood may be spilled here. However, it is a Celtic tradition to pit chosen champions against one another to decide a battle, rather than embark upon all-out war; such a great waste of manpower.'

I suppose that *does* make some sense' conceded Machinator. 'Our main task here is mining *plumbum*, not slaughtering Celts. Although we're not averse to a bit of slaughter.'

The Romans went into a huddle to discuss this proposal.

All right then' said the centurion, addressing the Druids. 'Choose your champion and we'll choose ours. We will meet back here tomorrow and settle this once and for all!'

The Romans then returned to the *plumbum* mines while the Dobunni tribesmen went off to make their offerings to their goddess Sul.

The following morning, the Romans and Celts met again at the clearing by the Sacred Spring. The Romans had chosen as their champion a huge, muscle-bound moron named Desperatus Danus. The Celts' champion was a man of similar build and intellect named Atox the Savage.

'Before the contest begins, explain this' said Cophinus Mucrus. 'If blood cannot be spilt here, how can the victor of the contest be determined?'

'The combatants may break each other's necks' replied Corsog the Druid.

'That seems fair enough.' Machinator conceded.

'However,' continued Corsog, 'in the Celtic tradition, before battle may commence, the champions have to hurl terrible verbal insults at each other! Their resulting rage will guarantee a ferocious fight to the death!'

'I like that idea!' enthused Mucrus.

The Romans and the Celts withdrew some distance, leaving the two huge combatants glaring at each other across the narrow clearing.

'You start, Atox!' called out Corsog. 'The home team always starts first.'

'Your mother is a goat!' shouted Atox; then waited for

Desperatus Danus' angry reaction. Nothing. The large Celt repeated the insult. Still nothing. It was little wonder that he didn't receive a reaction. All Desperatus Danus heard was: '*Maich mam yn afr!*' He did not understand a word of the local language!

'Our man is slow to anger' said Mucrus vaguely. 'It's your turn, Danus!' he called.

'Your father is a monkey's uncle!' he yelled at Atox. But of course all Atox heard was '*Simia patre patruus!*'

'Try again, Atox!' called Corsog.

'*Os ydych wedi cael meddwl beth fyddech chi'n ei wneud?*' was Atox's next offering. Danus just stood and stared. He did not realise that Atox had just asked him that if he, Danus, had a brain, what would he use it for?! Nevertheless, it was his turn now.

'Do you live in a pigsty? It smells like it!' said Danus.

Atox just looked blankly at the Roman. All he had heard was '*Tu habitas volutabrum? Sentit sicut eam!*'

And so it went on. Instead of the anticipated rising fury there was only total bewilderment and incomprehension!

The day wore on and the opponents became more and more weary as they exhausted their limited vocabularies. At last the Romans and Celts called a halt to this farce.

'We have to call the contest a draw,' said Corsog, 'or we will be here forever!'

'I have a suggestion' said the Druid Gywbedyn, who had said little up to this point. 'Why not combine our goddesses and dedicate the Sacred Spring to a new, local, Romano-Celtic goddess and name her Sulis Minerva?'

'That sounds reasonable,' said Cophinus Mucrus,

'however, I believe the goddess should be called Minerva Sulis.'

'I don't agree. We were here first' said Corsog. 'However, we could set up a new contest between our two worthy champions to decide this. Shall we?'

A resounding 'NO!' echoed around the Sacred Spring!

'... *And so it was settled*' said Lucidus to his discipuli. '*Sulis Minerva became the goddess of the waters that are now sacred to both Celts and Romans. Soon afterwards, the temple to the new goddess and the public baths were constructed. So although we Romans often prefer to use wholesale slaughter to get our way, sometimes we concede that compromise and diplomacy prove to be better solutions. That is the end of this story. Class dismissed!*'

Luridus – sallow, wan
Nasutus – long-nosed
Optrex – he had an eye for the ladies!
Mordax – biting, snappy
Inscritus – ignorant
Rhufeiniwr – Romans or strangers
Corsog – marshy, boggy
Gwybedyn – midge, gnat

IV.
Pavor in Aquae Sulis!
(Panic in Aquae Sulis!)

Lucidus, the schoolmaster, began that day's Tale with a little history lesson:

'The Emperor Hadrian, unlike his predecessors, was concerned about men and women sharing the same changing facilities at public baths, where they also bathed together – often in the nude. He wanted to discourage the inevitable temptations that such arrangements might lead to.

Therefore, he decreed that, henceforth, men and women should no longer share the same facilities, nor should they bathe together. Accordingly, separate changing areas would have to be built and separate bathing times arranged.

Now throughout the Empire, Roman men generally worked from early morning until mid-afternoon and therefore the women, who had no rights at all and generally didn't work (that was a slave's job!), had to fit in with these arrangements.

Thus, the women used the baths in the mornings, but would then have to vacate the baths when the men returned home from work. These new arrangements seem to have worked fairly well throughout the Empire, but, in Aquae Sulis, in the province of Britannia, they had different ideas!

Aquae Sulis was 1400 miles from Rome, so the local authorities, represented by Gaius Tiberinus, the General Overseer of the Complex, decided to ignore the Emperor's decree, reasoning that the chances of the Emperor Hadrian ever visiting Britannia were very slim. They would thus save themselves the cost of expensive rebuilding work. However...'

...Gaius Tiberinus, was reclining at the side of the Great Bath one afternoon, talking to his friend, the high priest, Gaius Calpurnius Receptus.

Tiberinus was quite short in stature and of decidedly robust physique (no-one would have *dared* call him fat – he was famous for his volatile temper!). His thinning hair was suspiciously dark for a man in his fifties.

By contrast, Receptus was tall and elegant with a calm, patrician face. He was also as bald as a badger.

Whilst they were exchanging pleasantries, Tiberinus' secretary, Halitus Malus, came rushing up breathlessly.

Malus was a tall skinny youth with a mop of bright red hair and vacant blue eyes. He had inherited the position of secretary to the Overseer from his father, who had recently retired due to mulsum-induced ill-health. (Mulsum being a strong alcoholic drink comprised of wine mixed with honey.)

'Master!' cried the secretary. 'We have just received a letter from Governor Falco in Londinium and it is great news! The Emperor Hadrian has landed in Britannia!'

Tiberinus spat out the oyster he was about to swallow and glared at Halitus. 'What!! You said it was *great* news!'

'It is great news, master; for all loyal subjects!'

'What, *both* of them?

'Pardon, master?'

'Oh, forget it!'

Tiberinus turned to the high priest as he wiped the oyster dribble from his chin. 'Now I'm for it' he groaned. 'For what?' asked the priest. 'What have you got to fear? Why the sweat?'

I've been sending letters to Rome reporting the progress of the conversion of the Baths, as per the Emperor's noble decree.'

'So?'

'We haven't moved so much as a brick!'

'Ah, I see your problem. I think sweating might be in order after all.'

'You're no help' moaned Tiberinus. 'What am I to do?'

'Start a programme of panic building. Right away!' replied the priest.

'That's easier said than done! Where can I get builders

at such short notice?'

'This looks like a job for young Belator' said Gaius Calpurnius Receptus.

Belator was a 16 year-old slave who had worked at the Baths almost all of his short life. He was highly intelligent, quick-witted and resourceful. His small, wiry frame and reddish-blonde hair hinted at foreign ancestry. He was always neat and clean and spoke quietly and politely to everyone. And Belator had a secret; a very great secret. He could both read and write Latin fluently!

'Malus!' said Tiberinus. 'Send Belator to me at once!'

'What? Belator the slave, master?'

'No. Belator the Emperor!'

'I thought Hadrian was the Emperor, master. Is he not?'

'Only in the mornings.'

'Really?'

'Oh, for the gods' sakes, fetch the slave!'

Halitus Malus rushed off shouting 'Belator! Belator!'

'I don't understand why you employ that moron' said the priest.

'Because he's cheap and he's the only one around here who can read and write, after a fashion, apart from Marcus Librerius the scribe, and *he's* kept busy all day writing out tablets to the goddess Sulis Minerva.'

'At least you could get the idiot to do something about his breath' said Receptus. 'It smells like a stable after the ponies have had the trots!'

A moment later Belator came running up.

'You sent for me, master?' he said.

'Yes' replied Tiberinus. 'I need masons and builders to do some quick work on the Baths and I need them now! You have lots of contacts; can you find me such people? There will be a purse in it for you if you can!'

'I think I can help, master, but they may not come cheap' replied the slave.

'Cost is no object; my neck is at stake!' replied Tiberinus.

'I'll need some money in advance to cover initial costs' said Belator.

'Yes. Anything! Anything!' said the desperate Tiberinus.

Armed with a bag of silver *denarii* (a denarius was worth about £10 in today's money), Belator set off into the town to find his friend and confederate, Devius.

Devius, like Belator, was a 16 year-old slave and, like Belator, was intelligent, quick-witted and, as his name suggests, devious. However, in appearance the two friends could not have been more different. Devius was a huge, untidy individual with broad shoulders and a mop of unruly black hair. He worked for a local blacksmith; hence he was always covered in dirt and sweat. His father swore that he would make a fine gladiator one day, but Devius had other plans.

Devius, like his friend Belator, could also read and write! This was almost unheard of in a slave, but Belator was a great favourite of the gentle scribe, Librerius, and the old man had secretly educated him. Librerius felt that Belator was destined for better things than a life of slavery. The arrangement worked well in the scribe's favour too;

as the old man's eyesight was slowly getting poorer and Belator was, more and more, becoming his eyes. The young slave would assist the scribe when not engaged in his normal chores around the Baths.

In turn, Belator had taught his friend Devius to read and write and with this advantage over even the most influential, but generally semi-literate Romans, the young rogues had devised and executed numerous money-making schemes!

When the lads met, Belator explained the task he had been set. 'You have an uncle who used to work as a slave for a master builder before he was made a *libertus* (freedman), don't you?' Belator asked his friend.

'That's right. My uncle Ebrius' replied Devius. 'He became a master builder himself after he was freed, but he spent too much time in the *taverna* with his builder buddies and in the end they all lost their jobs because of their devotion to Bacchus!'

'Well, if they can sober up long enough to perform one more building task, there will be enough money in it for them to spend the rest of their lives sprawled in the arms of Bacchus!'

Devius put the idea to his uncle Ebrius who signed up immediately.

Ebrius was a large man, like his nephew, and had a face that told the story of his dissolute life. He was famous for the exotic tattoos that festooned his large back and he needed little encouragement to strip off his shirt and display his erotica!

Ebrius rounded up his cronies and soon a large band of bleary, but keen, ex-builders presented themselves to Belator.

'I need some of you to purchase building materials and have them delivered to the Baths. Here is the list. I will pay for them personally on delivery' he added wisely.

The two young slaves then set about concocting suitable 'credentials', showing that Ebrius and his merry band of drunkards were some of the most reliable builders in Britannia! Then the lads went off to 'borrow' a suitable set of building plans from the *Curia* (town hall).

Ebrius copied these plans, making suitable alterations, before the originals were quietly returned to the archives.

The 'credentials' and plans were duly presented to Gaius Tiberinus, who approved them immediately. He congratulated Belator on his swift results and excused him his usual duties until the building was completed.

'I'm putting you in charge' said Tiberinus. 'The fewer people who know what's going on here the better!'

And so work began in understandably chaotic fashion, with Ebrius in overall charge of building, but with everyone under the control of Belator. Eventually order was established, the work settled down and rapid progress was made. Somehow, the young slave managed to keep Ebrius and his crew out of the *taverna* with a mixture of promised financial rewards and downright threats! (Librerius, the scribe, who knew what was going on, had prepared some gut-churning curses – just in case!)

Other professional builders and masons in Aquae Sulis were curious as to why such a large project was being overseen by a drunken ex-builder, who in turn took his orders from a 16 year-old slave; but they knew better than to question the instructions of the irascible Gaius Tiberinus.

Miraculously, the project was eventually completed in just over five weeks and the new edifice at the east end of the Baths was designated 'the Women's Baths'.

At last an ecstatic Tiberinus was able to send a letter to the Emperor, who was stationed in *Eboracum* (York), informing him that the work had been completed, as per his noble decree and that the Baths were ready for his inspection, should the divine Hadrian decide to honour Aquae Sulis with a visit.

The official opening took place one beautiful sunny day in front of a huge crowd, with the new edifice being blessed by the high priest, Gaius Calpurnius Receptus. Gaius Tiberinus made a lengthy and pompous speech:

'... And so, my friends, it gives me great pleasure to announce these splendid baths, open! May they stand for a thousand years!' he concluded.

'But they won't though, will they, Belator?' whispered Librerius, the scribe, to the young slave who was standing beside him.

'It's unlikely, master.'

'Be on your way then, lad' said the old man with a little smile.

Tiberinus kept his promise to Belator and gave him a handsome bonus for his efforts. Belator in turn, shared the purse with his friend Devius.

A well-paid Ebrius and his cronies crawled back into their favourite taverna and drank themselves into happy oblivion...!

Lucidus concluded his tale:

'Librerius the scribe was well aware that the new building could not possibly stand for a thousand years, or even for ten years, because the dissolute lifestyle of Ebrius the builder and his gang ensured that they were not nearly as competent as their credentials made them out to be and their workmanship consequently was of very poor quality.

Belator knew this too, but he also knew that even the shoddiest workmanship would save Tiberinus' skin – at least for the time being!
In fact, the new baths lasted for just over three years, before they collapsed in spectacular fashion! Thankfully, no-one was hurt.

Thus, Tiberinus had to have the Women's Bath completely rebuilt by competent builders at huge extra cost to himself. In the end he paid heavily for his laziness and dishonesty!'

PS. The Emperor Hadrian never did visit Aquae Sulis during his 3-months' stay in Britannia. His priorities were in subduing a Pict rebellion in the north and marking the Roman Empire's most northerly border by building the long barrier that became known as Hadrian's Wall.

However, there is a possible reason why the Emperor never did visit the Baths at Aquae Sulis. This is explained in the next tale...

V.
Hadrianus ad Balneis Agrippae
(Hadrian and the Baths of Agrippa)

Lucidus, the schoolmaster, began his next tale:

'The Emperor Hadrian built extensively throughout his 20-year reign. He also repaired and modernised many existing buildings and monuments. One such repair was carried out at the Baths of Agrippa in Rome. It is well known that the Emperor liked to be seen out and about by the ordinary Romans – it made him feel at one with his people – and one such opportunity was by bathing amongst them at the public baths.'

(NB. The source of the following tale comes from an actual document: HISTORIA AUGUSTA – HADRIAN, PART II.)

Gaius Suetonius Tranquillius, personal secretary to the Emperor Hadrian, gazed out of the window of his apartment across the rooftops of Rome. He loved this view and it always filled him with pride to know that he was a citizen of the Eternal City and a trusted confidante of the Divine Hadrian.

It had been a long, busy day and Suetonius was looking forward to a hot bath and a glass of his best wine, when his reveries were interrupted by the arrival of a messenger from the Imperial Palace.

'Master,' said the young man breathlessly. 'The Emperor desires your presence at the Palace. At once.'

'It's always "At once!"' muttered Suetonius, grabbing his cape and following the messenger out of the door.

Publius Aelius Triainus Hadrianus Augustus, Emperor of Rome, was in an expansive mood when his secretary came panting in.

'You sent for me, Divinity?' said Suetonius.

'Ah, my good Suetonius!' boomed the Emperor. 'Good of you to come!'

'As if I had a choice' thought the secretary.

Publius Aelius Triainus Hadrianus Augustus

Hadrian certainly was an impressive figure as he stood casually in front of his none-too-fragrant secretary. He was a tall, muscular man with carefully curled hair and, unlike his predecessors, sported a full beard. The Emperor loved all things Greek and accordingly had grown a beard in the style of the Greek philosophers. In fact, Hadrian had acquired the nickname 'Greekling' when he was younger.

'Now that the repair work on the Baths of Agrippa has been completed, I would like to go bathing there tonight' he said. 'Right now, in fact.'

'The baths will be full of ordinary citizens at this time of day, sire' ventured Suetonius.

'So much the better' replied Hadrian. 'The citizens of Rome will be pleased to see their Emperor among them.'

'I will order your carriage right away, sire' said the secretary.

And so, with his usual entourage of Praetorian Guards and numerous officials and attendants, the Emperor set off for the baths.

Once there, the ordinary citizens were kept at a respectful distance while the Emperor had scented oils rubbed into his body in the *tepidarium* (warm room), then he luxuriated in the fierce heat of the *caldarium* (hot steam room) before returning to the *tepidarium*, where trusted attendants scraped the oil from his body with golden *strigils* (scrapers). The other bathers were ushered to one side by the Praetorian Guard so that the Emperor could walk unimpeded to the great bath.

As he was about to enter the water, Hadrian noticed an old man rubbing his back against one of the columns that supported the huge barrelled roof of the baths. The Emperor recognised the man as one of the soldiers who had been on campaign with him years before. 'Why are you rubbing yourself against the column in that fashion?' he enquired.

'Divinity,' said the old soldier. 'I am a poor man now that I am no longer in your service. I cannot afford to pay a slave to clean me with his strigil, nor can I afford to rent a strigil myself, so I clean myself thus.'

Hadrian turned to his secretary. 'Suetonius, give this faithful old soldier some coins so that he may hire a slave to clean him properly.'

Suetonius dutifully handed the man some money from his own purse. 'I doubt I'll get any of that back.' he thought.

The old man took the money with grateful thanks and rushed off.

'I wish I could help all my old soldiers who have fallen on hard times' said the Emperor, as he watched the man go.

'He seems to be heading for the exit' observed Suetonius.

'He'll be back, I'm sure,' said Hadrian.

After an invigorating swim, watched from a distance by the admiring citizens of Rome, the Emperor, with his party in tow, returned to the Imperial Palace.

'That was most enjoyable' he said to Suetonius. 'Arrange for me to visit the baths again tomorrow.'

The following afternoon, the Royal party descended on the baths once again. Hadrian went through the usual oiling and scraping ritual, then headed for the great bath for a refreshing swim and once again the ordinary citizens were required to keep their distance from the Divine presence.

As the Emperor reached the water's edge, he suddenly stopped dead in his tracks. All around the great bath dozens of old men were diligently scraping their backs against the columns!

'What the...? The rogues! They've heard what transpired yesterday and are also looking for a handout! Do they think I'm a soft touch?' he snarled to Suetonius. 'Well I'll show them they don't mess with the Emperor of Rome!'

He raised his voice and called for silence.

'Listen, all you men!' he shouted. 'Do you think me stupid? Do you think I am going to fall for your tricks? If you cannot afford a slave with a strigil, then pair up and scrape each other clean!'

With that, Hadrian turned on his heel and stormed out of the baths, leaving the assembled bathers open mouthed!

He fumed all the way back to the palace.

'How dare they try to take advantage of my good nature! I wasted good money on that old fraud!'

'*You* didn't waste a *quadrans*' (a small coin of low denomination), thought Suetonius ruefully.

The Emperor Hadrian seemed to have lost his enthusiasm for bathing in public after that incident!

Licidus concluded his tale with this thought:

'It has been suggested that Hadrian never did use the Baths in Aquae Sulis during his visit to Britannia, because of his experience in Rome. However, we will never know for sure. Class dismissed!'

VI.
Nundinae
(Market day)

Lucidus started that day's Tale thus:

'As you know, most Roman towns and cities hold weekly markets where people come from far and wide to buy and sell their wares. It was at such a market in Aquae Sulis that the young slave, Belator, met the girl of his dreams!

At the Baths in Aquae Sulis, as with any public place, people are always losing things. Normally, records of lost property are kept and the list of items is long and varied. Things people often lose include: money, clothing, sandals, gloves, hats, rings, earrings, brooches, bracelets, wigs, false teeth and false limbs!

Belator had been made custodian of all lost property there. On one memorable occasion, he had saved his master, Gaius Tiberinus, from a situation that could have proved embarrassing, even fatal (see Tale IV), and so Tiberinus felt beholden to the young slave; hence the responsibility of looking after lost property at the Baths. Any lost property was kept for a period of time and, if unclaimed, was sold from a second-hand stall that Belator ran at the weekly market on behalf of Gaius Tiberinus.

However, before taking any clothing to market, Belator

would have it washed and, where necessary, repaired, by his mother, Clementina. This ensured a better selling price! He considered the extra money earned in this way as his 'perk'...'

Belator had erected the brightly-coloured awning over his market stall, which he had pitched as close to the centre of the market as he could manage. Trade was always better there. The young slave was busy laying out his wares, when his master, Gaius Tiberinus, hove into view, followed by his wife, Lady Flavia and her slave, Apulia.

Behind them, pushing a handcart lumbered another slave, Stultus, a huge, muscle-bound man with the intellect of an artichoke. Stultus had a childlike devotion to Tiberinus who used him as a personal bodyguard and general dogsbody.

Belator watched them approach.

'The old *bufo* (toad) is checking up on me!' he thought. However, Tiberinus did not stop at the stall. He had more important things to attend to.

As he passed, he called out to Belator. 'Make sure you get a good price for your wares, young man!'

'I will, master!' he replied. 'Better than you'll ever know, old man!' he added under his breath.

That morning Tiberinus and company were heading for the Slave Market. Lady Flavia had persuaded her husband that there was need of another female slave to help at the Baths and around their villa. Along the way they passed a *venditor de Eventus Maximus* (Big Issue seller). Flavia bought a copy, as was her habit. She liked to think that she was helping those less fortunate than herself.

The Slave Market was the usual mix of noise, raucous laughter, ribaldry and abject misery. The slave dealer was a huge, evil-smelling man called Ignoramus Maximus; and never was a name more appropriate! Above the rostrum where he auctioned the slaves he had erected a large sign which read: **BOSOF** (Buy One Set One Free) – (*as if!*)

Tiberinus, like everyone else, loathed this man and his dark sense of humour, but Ignoramus ran the only slave market in Aquae Sulis, so was tolerated by default.

'What am I bid for this fine young specimen?' bellowed the slave dealer.

By his side stood a scrawny lad of about 15 years of age, staring miserably at the ground. The bidding started slowly, but soon picked up and before long the youth was sold to a new master for 50 *sestertii*. (About £125 in today's money.)

'Next, I have this fine young maiden, fresh from the Greek Islands! Her name is Maria and she is 16 years old. This should put the roses back in the cheeks of some lucky bidder!' laughed Ignoramus.

Lady Flavia turned to her husband. 'We must buy that poor young wretch before someone like that grubby old *mustela* (weasel) over there does!'

She pointed to Libidinosus, a huge pot-bellied trader who had acquired quite a harem of young female slaves.

'Who will start the bidding?' yelled Ignoramus. 'Do I hear 100 sestertii? Seventy five? Fifty'

'Forty five sestertii' called out Libidinosus.

The young slave Maria stared out at the gathering. She

certainly was a beauty; small and slender with long black hair and huge dark brown eyes.

'Fifty sestertii' said Gaius Tiberinus.

Libidinosus glared at Tiberinus. He did not wish to be outbid for this prize. 'Sixty sestertii!' he countered.

Young Maria looked back and forth between the two bidders; her eyes pleading with Tiberinus to raise the bid.

'One hundred sestertii!' he called.

Libidinosus snarled and shook his head. He knew he could not outbid a rich man like Tiberinus.

'Sold to the esteemed Gaius Tiberinus!' crowed Ignoramus. He had just made a very handsome profit.

Tiberinus paid the slave dealer and beckoned to Maria. 'I am Gaius Tiberinus, Overseer of the Baths and Temple complex. This is where you will be put to work. This is my wife, the Lady Flavia. You will go with her now.' He did not bother to introduce the other slaves.

'Come with me, child' she said. 'We have shopping to do and you will help carry our purchases. Do you speak much Latin?' she enquired.

'I was taught Latin at school before I was enslaved, mistress' replied Maria.

'You went to school?' said a surprised Tiberinus. 'We Romans prefer our women to busy themselves with domestic chores and not to trouble their pretty little heads with education!'

Maria glared at him, but wisely said nothing.

With that, Tiberinus strolled off to attend to some other important matters.

On their way to the main market, Flavia and her

entourage passed Belator's stall again. Trade was brisk – Romans liked a good bargain – and as he looked up the young slave caught Maria's eye. His stomach gave a lurch. He had never seen such a beautiful girl. Belator turned to no-one in particular and said 'I'm going to marry that girl one day.'

Flavia's first stop was at the food stalls. Her husband had arranged a feast at their villa for some of the city's most prominent citizens and important visitors and Flavia had been tasked with buying in the food and drink for the forthcoming event.

Her first purchase; a dozen plump dormice! These were a great delicacy with rich Romans. The dormice would be fattened up with walnuts, acorns and chestnuts before they were killed and stuffed with pork sausage meat and flavoured with pepper and nuts.

The next purchase was a bag of live snails. These would be fed on milk until they were really fat before they were fried in oil and served in a wine sauce. A truly delicious appetizer!

Flavia continued with her shopping list, which included; song thrushes, herring gulls, ravens, jackdaws, swans, crows, storks and badgers. (Most Romans couldn't tell stork from badger.)

The party then moved on, with Stultus lumbering along behind pushing his now groaning hand cart.

They arrived at the stalls where makeup and perfumes were on sale. There Flavia bought some red ochre which would add an attractive rosy tinge to her cheeks.

As all Roman women of class were expected to have smooth legs and arms, Flavia then purchased a quantity of expensive hair remover. Her favourite potion was made from the blood of a wild she-goat, mixed with powdered viper and sea-palm. This would be applied liberally to the areas to be exfoliated. After a few more purchases, Flavia and her party made their way home to the Tiberinus villa.

At the end of the market day, Belator closed down his stall and returned to the Baths. He took his earnings and laid them out on the table in Gaius Tiberinus' office.

'A good day today, master!' he said. 'The stall took a great deal of money. This fine weather always brings out the buyers.'

'Well done, Belator' said Tiberinus. 'Now return to your normal duties.'

As Belator walked along the side of the Great Bath he passed his mentor, Librerius, the scribe.

'Did you sell well today, Belator?' the old man asked.

'Very well indeed, master' Belator replied.

'And you handed all your earnings to Gaius Tiberinus, I presume?'

'Well, yes. Less my commission, of course!' grinned the young slave.

'Be on your way, you young rogue' smiled the scribe.

As he was walking away, Belator suddenly stopped and called back to Librerius. 'By the way, master. Today I met the girl I'm going to marry one day, with the permission of my master, of course.'

'And I truly believe you will, young Belator' said the old man quietly.

VII.
Cenerat in villa de Tiberinus
(Dining at the Tiberinus villa)

Addressing his discipuli, Lucidus described in detail how rich Romans prepared their feasts:

'One day, Gaius Tiberinus and his wife, Lady Flavia Tiberina, were preparing to throw a dinner party at their villa for a number of their friends and for a special guest of honour, Aulius Platorius Nepos, the newly-appointed governor of Britannia, who was staying at the home of Tiberinus for a few days. Nepos had come down from Londinium to bathe in the sacred waters and to make a sacrifice to the goddess, Sulis Minerva. He had a special interest in consulting with his old friend and fellow dinner guest, Lucius Marcius Memor, who was the only Britannia-based Haruspex ('gut gazer' and augurer). The Governor was anxious to do well in his important new post and wanted the Haruspex to read the portents for him in the entrails of a fine young ox that Nepos had brought with him. He wanted to know if his plans and ambitions would *find favour with the gods.*

His host, Tiberinus, was the General Overseer of the Baths and the Temple complex in Aquae Sulis. He was a very important man and his dinner parties were legendary. (Actually, Gaius, being a typical Roman man, took no part whatsoever in the organising of a party; that was woman's work according to him!).

His wife, Lady Flavia, spent the morning rushing here and there in a great state of agitation, ordering her slaves and servants about. There was so much to do and so little time!'...

'Maria! Apulia! Where are those wretched girls? They're never here when I want them!' fumed Lady Flavia, as she paced around the *triclinium* (dining room).

Maria came panting up, covered in flour. A moment later, Apulia arrived. She was covered in soot and ash.

'Where have you been! What have you been up to?' cried Flavia.

'Making bread and biscuits as you ordered, mistress' said Maria.

'Cleaning out the furnaces and the *hypocaust* (underfloor heating system) as you ordered, mistress' replied Apulia.

'Well, never mind that now! Send Salmonellus, the *coquus* (cook) to me. I want to run through tonight's menu again.' The slave girls obediently ran off to the *culina* (kitchen) to fetch Salmonellus. When he arrived he had a large sheaf of recipes under his arm.

'Salmonellus,' said Flavia. 'Remind me again what dishes

we are preparing for our guests.'

'Well, mistress,' said the *coquus*, with a hint of a Gallic accent. 'For *gustatio* (starters), we have a variety of delicacies: eggs, fish, olives, salad, mushrooms and oysters.'

'That doesn't seem much' said Flavia. 'Add a few more items.'

'Yes mistress. Now for *primae mensalae* (main course) we have seven dishes. These will include fish, meat, poultry, vegetables, dates, roast songbird, lamb's innards stuffed with sausage meat, snails fattened in milk and fried in oil and finally, stuffed dormice cooked in honey and poppy seeds; as well as lashings of *garum* (fish sauce), and of course, to drink, copious amounts of *mulsum* (honeyed wine).'

'Make sure there is plenty of everything. My guests have very healthy appetites' said Lady Flavia.

'We also have certain other delicacies in reserve, if you require them, mistress.'

'Such as?'

'Sheep's brains, goat's lungs, horsemeat sausages, egg custard with nettles stewed in seaweed, swan, stork and badger, mistress.

'Have these prepared and ready, just in case' said Flavia. 'Yes mistress. There may be need of some *vomitae paterae* (vomit bowls) to be laid by, in that case' replied Salmonellus.

'Yes, almost certainly. See to it. Now, what have we for *secundae mensae* (dessert)?' asked Flavia.

'Fresh and dried fruit seasoned with pepper and

honey, and still more *mulsum*, just in case the honoured guests wish to take part in an *acommissatio* (drinking contest)' said the *coquus*.

'Good! Now be about your work and *hurry*!' said Flavia, as she dismissed Salmonellus.

With the villa being cleaned and the food being prepared, Flavia turned her attention to the guest list. She sent for Moribundus, the ancient *nomenclator* (usher), who kept the list.

Moribundus was an ex-slave, of Greek origin. He was tall and stooped and wore a look of perpetual bewilderment on his face. He was considered by many to be the oldest man in Aquae Sulis, though no-one really knew his age. He had served the father of Gaius Tiberinus for many years and was retained as an usher out of sympathy rather than for his usefulness.

'We have seven guests, plus the master and me, so that makes nine diners tonight' she said to the old man, 'so there will be three people per *triclinia* (dining couch). A perfect number of diners.' (Flavia was proud of her numeracy).

'Let us check the guest list again' she instructed Moribundus.

'Apart from you and the master, there's His Excellency the governor, Aulius Platorius Nepos and his wife the Lady Stulta; the high priest, Gaius Calpurnius Receptus and his wife Trifosa Calpurnia; the Haruspex, Lucius Marcius Memor, and his wife Voluptua and finally Noelius Covardus (pronounced Cowardus); he has no wife, as you know.'

In the early afternoon, as pre-arranged, the dinner guests met at the Baths where they bathed in the hot waters and were pampered by their slaves before being taken by carriage to the Tiberinus villa.

They alighted in front of the *atrium* (villa hallway), where they were met by Moribundus the usher.

'Dinner is about to be served, masters' he said, as he collected the cloaks, shawls and shoes from the party.

'Would you do me the honour of being the first to cross my threshold, Excellency?' said Tiberinus to Governor Nepos.

'That would be my pleasure' replied Nepos, as he made to cross the threshold with his left foot.

A sharp, communal intake of breath stopped him in his tracks.

'Right foot first, my dear. Always!' hissed his wife, the Lady Stulta.

'Oh. I forgot. My apologies' he muttered and corrected his, literal, *faux pas*.

The guests were shown to their respective *triclinia* and settled down to dine.

As the food was brought out, Tiberinus noticed that one of the *ministrators* (waiters) was the young slave boy, Belator, who normally worked at the Baths. Tiberinus was beholden to the slave after Belator had saved his neck when the Overseer had ignored a decree from the Emperor Hadrian, ordering modifications to the Baths. (*See Tale IV.*)

Since that time, Tiberinus was always cautious in the presence of Belator. The slave knew too many secrets and was, without doubt, the most intelligent person in the Temple complex.

As if on cue, Governor Nepos, who was a personal friend of the Emperor Hadrian, turned to Tiberinus and said, 'That reminds me; before I left Rome, the Divine Hadrian said that he had heard that part of the Great Baths had collapsed recently. The Emperor expressed his hope that no-one had been injured.'

'Uh. No. Thank the gods' mumbled Tiberinus. 'Repairs have been effected and the Baths are stronger than ever.' (This wouldn't have been difficult, given the circumstances!)

'The Emperor will be pleased!' enthused Nepos. 'What exactly happened?'

But before Tiberinus had a chance to come up with a story, and to his immense relief, the dancers and musicians appeared and began to perform for the party. Nepos turned his attention to Noelius Covardus, who was at that moment admiring the physique of one of the young male musicians who was playing the pan pipes.

'I see you have not brought your wife with you this

evening, Covardus. I trust she is not indisposed?'

'I'm between partners at the moment, Excellency.' (An image that made him shudder with pleasure!)

The Governor pondered this enigmatic response for a moment, then addressed the Haruspex, Lucius Marcius Memor.

'As you know, Marcius, I have brought an ox to be slaughtered on the morrow so that I might know if my plans for the Province will find favour with the gods. I trust you will read the entrails for me?'

'It will be an honour to do so, Excellency' replied the Haruspex.

However, Marcius was not as confident as he sounded. Despite being one of only sixteen haruspices in the whole Empire, he was still fairly new at the job and had never been called upon to slaughter anything as large as an ox before. Chickens, geese, sheep, goats and sundry rodents, yes; but never an ox! He would need to consult with someone. But who? Then his eyes fell upon Belator, who was serving at the next *triclinia*.

Of course! Marcius knew, as did everyone else, that the brilliant young slave had saved old Tiberinus' neck some time ago.

'Belator?' he called.

'Yes, master?'

'I would speak with you in the morning. Meet me by my altar in the Temple Courtyard at first light.'

'Yes, master.'

The evening wore on, and as each course was served and the *mulsum* consumed in heroic quantities, the dinner guests became more voluble and less inhibited.

Towards the end of the *primae mensalae,* several of the guests, both male and female, felt the need to make room for more courses and so the *vomitae paterae* were passed around. Suddenly, Governor Nepos gave an enormous *ructus* (belch) which was greeted by a round of applause! This lead to a chorus of answering belches as the guests tried to outdo one another! This was perfectly acceptable in polite Roman society.

'That was spectacular!' cried Nepos. 'Did you know that the Emperor Claudius once considered passing an edict decreeing that 'other bodily emissions' might be acceptable in polite society? Regrettably, it never became law.' This piece of information was met with some solemn nodding of heads.

As midnight approached, the dinner guests had eaten and drunk enough to sink a good-sized galley and so they decided that it was time that they staggered off to bed! Carriages were called and the guests who had to travel home were poured into them and with loud 'Goodnights!' they rumbled off into the night. The hosts and their house guests crawled off to their respective *cubiculae* (bedrooms).

With the diners gone, it was time for the slaves and servants to begin the cleaning-up process. The mess was considerable! There was spilled drink and half-eaten food everywhere and the contents of the *vomitae paterae* had slopped all over the floor, so mops and buckets had to be fetched. While everyone else was busy sweeping and mopping, Belator took the opportunity to introduce himself to the beautiful young slave girl Maria. He had not had the chance to speak to her since he first saw and fell in love with her in the market place a few days before. He thought he would use a little wit to try and impress her.

'Good evening. I've been wanting to meet you. My name is Belator the Forgetful.'

'Oh, why do they call you that?' asked Maria shyly.

'Why do they call me what?' replied Belator.

Maria looked down and began to snigger, then she burst out laughing.

'You are funny!' she giggled.

'That's an encouraging start' thought Belator.

The young couple chatted well into the night as they helped tidy the Tiberinus villa.

The next morning, before Belator went off to meet

with the Haruspex, he related the previous evening's events to his mentor, the elderly scribe Librerius.

'By the end of the evening some of the honoured guests had regrettably lost their dignity' he said. 'They were bloated, covered in drink stains and bits of food and talking complete nonsense. Their brains seem to have been reduced to mush!'

'Ah' said the scribe. 'The indignity of over-indulgence. Always remember, my boy; *mens sana in corpore sano!*' (A healthy mind in a healthy body!)'

'I will remember that, master' said the young slave.

VIII.
Fons Sancta
(The Sacred Spring)

Lucidus started that day's tale with an explanation as to what a haruspex, or augurer, actually did:

'A Haruspex is a priest who reads the entrails, particularly the liver, of a newly sacrificed animal. He not so much foretells the future as divines whether the gods will approve or disapprove of some proposed course of personal, political or military action. There are only sixteen haruspices in the whole Empire, so we are fortunate to have one here in Britannia.

When not reading the portents, the haruspex usually keeps a number of chickens. When he feeds them grain he can also interpret the wishes of the gods. If the chickens eat the grain then the signs are good, but if they don't, then watch out!'...

The sun was slowly rising over the town of Aquae Sulis as young Belator the slave made his way across the Temple Courtyard towards the altar of Lucius Marcius Memor, the local Haruspex. Memor was already there waiting for him. He was looking decidedly the worse for wear and was obviously feeling the effects of the previous night's wining and dining at the villa of Bath's Overseer, Gaius Tiberinus. His normally gaunt features had a grey tinge to them in the early morning light.

'Ah, there you are!' he said, as Belator approached. Then without further preamble he continued. 'You no doubt heard last night that His Excellency, Governor Nepos, has brought an ox for me to slaughter today, so that I might read the portents from its entrails.'

'Yes, master. I heard.'

'Well, I have a problem' continued the Haruspex. 'I have not been a Haruspex for very long and am still learning my trade, so to speak. The fact is; although I am adept at slaughtering and reading the entrails of smaller animals, I have never slaughtered anything as large as an ox before! I'm afraid that I might make a hash of the whole ceremony! I've heard you are a resourceful lad, Belator. What can you suggest? You'll find I'm not ungenerous if you can help.'

The young slave pondered for a moment.

I think I may be able to help, master' he said, to the almost palpable relief of the Haruspex.

'I knew you could!' cried Memor, clapping his hands.

This noisy outburst drew disapproving looks from other early risers who were crossing the Temple Courtyard.

In a more subdued tone he continued, 'Well, tell me what your ideas are.'

'I have a friend, Marcus Lanius, who is a freedman and a professional butcher. His premises are not far from here. For a fee I'm sure he could dispatch the animal for you in his own slaughterhouse, quickly and efficiently. Then I could bring the liver to you before the appointed time of the Governor's arrival. You could tell His Excellency that you had dispatched the animal earlier so that you could read the portents in its entrails the moment he arrived, thus he would not be long delayed before going off to deal with the many other pressing matters that must await a man of his importance.'

'Capital! Capital!' cried Memor, once again drawing frowns from passers-by. 'See that this is done! Here is a purse for your butcher friend. Now go and fetch the ox from Gaius Tiberinus' cowshed.'

An hour or so later, His Excellency, Governor Aulius Platorius Nepos, arrived in the Temple Courtyard with his entourage. He too was looking a little fragile; his usual ruddy complexion was decidedly whey-coloured. At least he was on his feet, unlike his still-recumbent host, Gaius Tiberinus!

He found Lucius Marcius Memor standing by his altar,

holding the still-warm liver of the slaughtered ox in his hands. The Haruspex explained what had transpired. He then blessed the liver, intoning some mysterious prayers. He solemnly slit the liver open and gazed inside. Everyone stood around in respectful silence as the Haruspex read the portents, nodding his head and grunting from time to time. At last he raised his head and addressed the anxious Nepos.

'The best of news, Excellency!' he said. The portents could not be better! The gods smile upon you and will bless your every endeavour with good fortune!'

'This is wonderful news! My deepest thanks for your readings, my dear Memor!' said the Governor, as he shook the Haruspex enthusiastically by the hand. 'Here is a token of my gratitude!' and he handed Memor a hefty purse.

With that, the Governor and his wife stode off to their waiting carriage and were gone in an instant.

Memor opened the purse and poured a generous portion of it into the hands of Belator, who had handed him the ox liver moments before the arrival of the governor.

'This whole incident is between you and me only. Do you understand, Belator?' he said.

'Of course, master' said the young slave, as the Haruspex walked off with his head held high. He felt that he had handled a potentially embarrassing situation particularly well.

However, all was not what it seemed.

The liver that Memor had examined was *not* that of Nepos' fine young ox! That animal had been sold by the butcher and Belator to a local farmer as breeding stock! They received an excellent price, which they shared between them. The liver that the Haruspex had studied had actually belonged to an ancient ox that had been slaughtered for dog meat!

Belator was certain that most, if not all, of Memor's predictions were pure fabrications anyway. He felt sure that Nepos' fate would be decided by the gods, one way or another, irrespective of what the Haruspex had claimed to have read in the ox liver!

As ever, Belator's mentor, the elderly scribe, Librerius – who had spies everywhere – learned of his young friend's latest enterprise. He said nothing, but thought to himself: 'Woe to ye who would make slaves of those who are far more intelligent than ye are!'

IX.
Mane de Feminas ad Balneis
(Ladies' Morning at the Baths)

Lucidus, the schoolmaster, began that day's tale by describing what would happen on a typical day at the Roman Baths. Children were not allowed to use the Baths in those days...

A few days after the Tiberinus' dinner party, when everyone had fully recovered from the excesses of the evening, the fashionable ladies of Aquae Sulis met at the Great Bath, as was their custom every *Dies Veneris* (Venus Day, i.e. Friday).

The self-appointed leader of these 'ladies' mornings' was Lady Flavia Tiberina, wife of the powerful General Overseer, Gaius Tiberinus. The other ladies in attendance were Ammonia, Voluptua, Garrula, Maculosa, Obesita and Tibia and Fibula (two rather bony sisters). These ladies came in all shapes and sizes, but they had certain things in common; they were all extremely dim, vain and snobbish and very fond of the most scandalous gossip!

However, they came from patrician backgrounds and had married well, so they lived lives of indolent leisure.

One noticeable absentee was Trifosa Calpurnia, wife of the High Priest, Gaius Calpurnius Receptus. She was never invited to these gatherings for the simple reason that she was low-born and therefore, in the eyes of the Ladies, common. Trifosa had been a slave at the Temple when Calpurnius had met and fallen in love with her. He bought her freedom and married her more than twenty years ago, but she had never been fully accepted by the ladies. The fact that she was a good-hearted, gentle and friendly soul cut no ice with them.

Attending to the ladies' every needs were Flavia's two slave girls, Apulia and Maria. Maria was the girlfriend of Belator, the young slave who worked at the Great Bath. She regularly memorised all the gossip that she heard around her so that she could relay it to Belator. He would then store any potentially useful titbits that might one day be useful to him!

On that particular morning, the main topic of conversation was *cultus* (beauty matters), such as *lenocinium* (makeup), perfume and *gemmae* (jewellery).

Some of the wealthier ladies had brought along their own *cosmetae* (slave girls who specialised in beautifying their mistresses). The others hired the services of the resident *cosmetae*.

Flavia and some of the other ladies had been born in Rome and consequently were not truly fair-skinned. This was a matter of concern to them because pure white skin was an indication that one belonged to the leisure classes and did not indulge in common manual labour!

'I use a very expensive but very effective skin-lightening lotion on my face and hands' purred Flavia. 'I'm sure you can see what a difference it makes.'

Her colleagues politely nodded their agreement.

'It is made with the finest oils and herbs, but the main ingredient is actually chalk,' she continued. 'My mother, Vetula Putrida, prefers white lead to chalk. She says that white lead is far more nutritious for the skin and intends to use it every day for the rest of her life.' (And so she did; consequently shortening her life considerably!)

Flavia went on, 'I have a secret I will share with you. I use a bedtime skin potion, which, as you can see, helps maintain my beauty. I rub my face in the sweat from sheep's wool!'

This was met by a chorus of diplomatic 'Oohs' and 'aahs'.

The ladies continued to exchange beauty tips for a while. The list of makeup ingredients was long and impressive. It included; sheep excrement, placenta, vinegar, animal urine, blood, powdered viper, sulphur, ground oyster shells, poultry fat, bile, beeswax, red lead, mulberry juice, rose petals, wine dregs and gladiator sweat (the Great smell of Brutus!).

As the morning wore on, the ladies finally exhausted their discussion about makeup and moved on to another of their favourite topics: Gossip!

One of their regular targets was the gentle Trifosa Calpurnia. Lady Ammonia started the assault. She considered herself Flavia's deputy. She was a tall, thin woman with a disdainful and haughty air and an acid tongue. Her husband, acting-centurion Marcus Aufidius Maximus, was a man who had spent his married life trying to please his wife. He usually failed.

Ammonia lowered her voice in theatrical fashion: 'I've heard it said that, although Trifosa is the wife of a priest; for five days a week her body is a temple, but at the weekend it's an amusement park!'

This scandalous lie brought screeches of laughter from the other ladies.

'And I've also heard that our High Priest isn't as high as he might think he is either!' exclaimed Ammonia, warming to the subject. 'The rumour is that, despite his age, he still enjoys chasing after young girls!'

'Scandalous!' chorused the indignant ladies, to this equally untrue piece of gossip.

'However,' she continued, 'What's the harm? Dogs

chase chariots down the street, but they can't catch them either!'

Again, this was met with loud shrieks of laughter.

Maria the slave girl, standing a little way off, made a mental note to report this conversation to Belator. He was very fond of the High Priest and his wife and it was never a good idea to insult people whom Belator respected! It could safely be assumed that the gossiping ladies and Ammonia in particular, would move to the top of Belator's 'hit list'!

Oblivious to the fact that they were making a dangerous enemy, the ladies gossiped on into the afternoon, until it was time for them to retire to the *tepidarium* (warm room) for some serious pampering.

As they floated off to the tepidarium, Ammonia said to Obesita, 'You know, there are times when all this gossiping just bores me. I sometimes wish something exciting would happen from time to time.'

Maria, who was following close behind, whispered to herself, 'It will, dear lady. It surely will – and soon!'

Later that day, Maria dutifully reported to Belator all that she had heard. 'Remind me, Maria, my love,' said Belator, 'Ammonia is married to acting-centurion Marcus Aufidius Maximus is she not?'

Maria confirmed this.

'Aufidius Maximus must have some very influential friends. It's very rare for soldiers to be allowed to marry,' mused Belator. 'I wonder…' He did not elaborate as he wandered off.

A week or so later, Lady Ammonia was preening

herself in front of her mirror, when her husband burst into the room.

'Ammonia, light of my life!' he cried. 'I have just received some wonderful news!'

'You're getting an increase in salary?' said his wife hopefully.

She had recently felt that she needed a new wardrobe and in her mind's eye she had already spent any extra money that Maximus might earn!

'Better than that, my love! A promotion – to full centurion! The Haruspex has read the signs and the gods have favoured me!'

'How wonderful!' cried Ammonia. This would mean even more money!

'I take up my new post with the VI Legion Victrix early next week, so we must start packing right away!' said Maximus.

'We're moving? Where to?' asked Ammonia.

Already she could imagine herself mingling with the fine ladies of *Londonium*, *Camulodunum* or *Eboracum* (London, Colchester, York). Although she enjoyed the social life in Aquae Sulis, she felt it was just a bit too parochial for a fine lady such as herself.

'We're moving north!' said Maximus.

'Ah. Eboracum. How delightful!'

'No. I am to command a century and guard the new wall that holds back the savage Picts' replied her husband.

'The wall? The wall that the Emperor Hadrian built?' said Ammonia incredulously.

'The very same' exclaimed her husband. 'What an honour!'

'What an honour?' shrieked his wife. 'Stuck in some god-forsaken bog in the middle of nowhere!'

'Not *nowhere*, my dear' replied Maximus, somewhat perplexed by his wife's reaction. 'It's the most northerly boundary of the whole Empire and I'm to guard it.'

'But – but where will we live?' asked his despairing wife. 'Will we have a villa, slaves, an orchard?'

'No. But we'll have comfortable quarters in the main garrison' replied Maximus. 'Imagine me; a full centurion!'

'A fool centurion, more like!' yelled his wife, as she hurled a vase at his head.

Maximus executed a tactical retreat with as much dignity as he could muster. Ammonia was left alone to nurse her anguish. 'Quarters in a grubby garrison!' she wailed. 'I'll die! I need society! Society needs me! I'll protest! I won't go!'

However, the gods had spoken and there was no going back.

The following week, the fashionable ladies of Aquae Sulis gathered at Ammonia's villa to bid her farewell and wish her safe journey to the Wild North.

'She is so sad to be leaving us' said Lady Flavia. 'We'll miss her.' Not everyone present shared that sentiment. However, they all put on suitably sad faces and wished the distraught Ammonia Godspeed as they hugged her and kissed her tear-stained face.

The wagons containing all her worldly goods rumbled off on the long road north, with a sobbing Ammonia following behind in her carriage. Maximus rode ahead, as befitted a centurion of the Roman army.

None of the fashionable ladies ever found out that Ammonia's departure had been engineered by the crafty Belator! A few days before, Belator had relayed what Maria had told him to Gaius Tiberinus and Gaius Calpurnius Receptus. Tiberinus was outraged at the way the ladies had gossiped about the wife of his good friend Receptus.

'If I may make a suggestion, masters' said Belator. 'I understand that a centurion's post has become available in the VI Legion Victrix in the North. Perhaps the honourable Marcus Aufilius Maximus might be the best man for the job. I'm sure his Excellency Governor Nepos could be persuaded to authorise the necessary paperwork.'

'Good thinking, Belator!' crowed Tiberinus.

And so it came to pass.

Neither Tiberinus nor Receptus thought to ask Belator where he had acquired his information. They really didn't want to know.

'There is a moral to this episode, you know,' Tiberinus said to his friend. 'Gossiping has a habit of coming back to bite you!' Receptus nodded wisely in agreement.

X.
Post Meridiem de Hominum ad Balneis
(Men's Afternoon at the Baths)

Lucidus' next tale related how the men enjoyed themselves when it was their turn to use the Great Bath in the afternoons...

As was their custom on *Dies Veneris* (Venus Day, i.e. Friday), the General Overseer of the Temple and Great Bath Complex, Gaius Tiberinus and some of his cronies, Noelius Covardus, Gaius Receptus, Marcus, Lucius, Gayus, Solar Plexus, Nausius and Bilius, were lounging around the Great Bath eating, drinking and indulging in man-talk (male gossip). As ever, the young slave, Belator, was in attendance.

'Fetch us some oysters, slave!' bellowed Nausius 'and be quick about it, you young loafer!'

With that he threw a silver denarius at Belator.

The others in the group exchanged glances but said nothing. Nausius was new to Aquae Sulis, having just arrived from Londinium, but he was already known for his abrasive and high-handed manner. Being a newcomer, he had not yet learned that treating Belator in such a contemptuous and off-hand way would almost certainly have repercussions. In this instance, retribution was about to be swift and spectacular.

Belator turned without a word and walked over to Victor, the oyster seller, and ordered four dozen oysters. As he paid Victor, he isolated six of the oysters, took a tiny vial from his pouch and poured a few drops of a dark green liquid into each oyster. He then marked each one with a tiny red spot. 'Ensure that the marked oysters are put on the plate of the honourable Nausius' he instructed Victor.

The oyster seller went over to the party and placed six oysters on each man's plate, making sure that Nausius received the six marked ones.

Tiberinus and his friends began cracking open the oysters and devouring them with relish. They then washed down their meal with heroic quantities of *mulsum* and began to discuss the matters of the day.

Noelius Covardus, the acknowledged sage, philosopher, wit, *bon viveur* and habitué of the exercise yard, spoke first. Covardus was a tall, elegant man who tried to disguise his encroaching baldness with a bad comb-over. He considered himself the natural successor to Caius Petronius, the self-appointed leader of fashion and decorum who had lived in the time of the Emperor Nero. Covardus started by extolling the virtues of fine wine.

'Wine, my dear friends,' he drawled, 'is sunlight held together by water! It is poetry in a goblet!'

'Always to be taken in moderation, of course' counselled Bilius.

'Moderation. Pah!' countered Noelius. 'My dear boy, when I read about the evils of drink, I gave up reading!'

'But too much consumption of strong drink can leave one with a dreadful hangover' persisted Bilius.

'Ah, yes indeed! The Wrath of Grapes' said Noelius wisely. (*Apologies to John Steinbeck.*)

'I hear young Sulinus the stonemason is having to get married' observed Marcus, changing the subject.

'Having to?' queried Lucius.

'Yes. You know… a case of wife or death.'

'The wedding will be in the first week in *Iunius* (June)' added Tiberinus. 'Any later than that and the bride would have to be carried to the altar!'

Suddenly, Nausius interrupted the conversation with an almighty belch.

'Pardon me!' he apologised. 'I'm feeling a little queasy.'

'Perhaps it was somebody you ate' sneered Tiberinus. He was not a great fan of Nausius.

'I think I may have to… Oh, gods!' cried Nausius, jumping up and charging towards the *latrina* (toilet), scattering bathers like ninepins as he went!

As if by magic, Belator appeared at the table, scooped up the empty oyster shells from the party's plates and took them back to Victor for disposal. Tiberinus gazed thoughtfully after the young slave but said nothing.

'Anyway, about Sulinus,' he said to the group. 'Does anyone know who the lucky girl is?'

'I believe it is the ample and not-so-lovely Hirsuta' said young Solar Plexus.

This caused a communal dropping of jaws.

'What! The daughter of Medusa Vehemens?' cried Tiberinus.

'The very same.'

'The poor lad should have gone to *Lunetas Conservas* (Specsavers)' observed Tiberinus. 'He is gaining one large hairy spouse and a vulture for a *socrus* (mother-in-law)!'

'Not a vulture' observed Noelius. 'A vulture waits until you're dead before it eats your heart out.'

'Poor Sulinus.'

'Poor, poor, Sulinus.'

'What should we get him for a wedding present?' asked Solar Plexus.

'A one-way passage to Gaul might be appropriate' said Marcus.

The group fell silent for a moment as they pondered the fate of Sulinus.

'Ah. Here comes Nausius' said Bilius.

They all glanced up as Nausius wobbled back towards their table. He was a funny colour.

'Feeling any better?' asked Tiberinus.

'I think I... I... Oh, no!' and he vanished again; once more ploughing through the startled bathers.

Gayus, who had also gone to the latrines, returned and said to the company, 'I would postpone any visits to the latrines at the moment, if I were you.' He did not elaborate.

Belator came up with a pitcher of mulsum and started to refill the group's goblets. Tiberinus stared at him through narrowed eyes, but the slave's face was a mask.

'*Nunc est bibendum!*' exclaimed Noelius. ('Now's the time to drink!')

'I have a puzzle for you, Noelius,' said Bilius, anxious to get the conversation going again, 'Why do you think the gods invented women?'

The sage thought for a moment before replying – he was not known for his sympathy towards women.

'A strange question, but I believe it is because sheep, pigs and goats can't cook, fetch water or pour wine!'

This was met with a roar of laughter – although everyone looked around first, to make sure that no women were within earshot!

However, Belator *was* within earshot and would

almost certainly use this piece of male chauvinist piggery to his own advantage at a later date!

The conversation moved on to the recent visit of the Governor of Britannia, Aulius Platorius Nepos.

'I wonder if Lucius Marcius Memor's glowing predictions about his Excellency's future would have been quite so rosy if they had not been such good friends' mused young Solar Plexus.

'What are you inferring?' said Tiberinus sternly.

'Nothing' replied the young man. 'It just strikes me as strange that the noble Governor has had a string of bad luck since his return to Londinium, despite the gods' assurances of good fortune. Firstly, his favourite horse, Pegasus, died; keeled over, just like that. Secondly, his honourable wife, the Lady Stulta, whose intellect regrettably does not match her great beauty, got her *palla* (scarf) caught in the wheel of her husband's chariot and was dragged through the streets like a rag doll before they could free her. She sustained a broken arm and a total loss of dignity. Thirdly, and most importantly, his friend, the Divine Hadrian, has told him that the building progress of the northern wall is not satisfactory and that there may well be repercussions. The Emperor made it clear that he holds Nepos responsible.'

'These things happen' added Tiberinus. 'Perhaps the gods just changed their minds. That is their prerogative.'

At that moment, Belator appeared at Tiberinus' side.

'Forgive me, master,' he said, 'but I have just heard that the noble Nausius has been taken home in a carriage. Apparently, his humours were seriously out of balance.'

'Thank you, Belator' said Tiberinus. 'Let me have reports on his progress.'

As he watched the young slave depart, Gaius Tiberinus could not help but wonder if Belator had in some way been instrumental in Nausius's sudden and violent illness. He was well aware that it was Belator who had engineered the departure of the obnoxious Lady Ammonia to the wilds of the far North. Tiberinus was in no doubt that Belator, even though he was a slave, could be a dangerous adversary if provoked.

He was shaken out of his musings by someone tapping on his shoulder. It was the young athlete, Gayus.

'Do you think it might have been the oysters that made poor Nausius ill?' he enquired anxiously. 'Might we not all fall ill?'

'I think it unlikely' said Tiberinus. 'And in any case, we'd be showing symptoms by now, don't you think?'

The conversation moved on to the recent departure of Lady Ammonia.

'She didn't seem too keen on moving north with her husband' observed Receptus. 'She never had a good word to say about Aquae Sulis and yet, when she had to leave, she was in floods of tears. Strange woman.'

'Yes, indeed' agreed the company.

Talk turned, inevitably, to the dramatic exit of the unfortunate Nausius.

'He was purging the excess of yellow bile when last I saw him' said Gayus. 'That should help him regain the balance of his humours.'

'Perhaps he should be careful of what he orders

to eat in future – and how he orders it' said Tiberinus enigmatically.

His gaze turned again to Belator, who was standing by with a look of pure innocence on his face.

XI.
Nocte ad Amphitheatrum
(A Night at the Amphitheatre)

That day's tale, as told by Lucidus, was designed to warn his discipuli about the dangers of over-indulgence...

To celebrate Sulinus' forthcoming (enforced) marriage, some of his friends and colleagues had arranged a stag night for him with a visit to the amphitheatre, followed by an *acommissatio* (drinking contest) at their favourite watering hole, the *Male Psittacus* (Sick Parrot) tavern.

The play that was being performed was 'A Funny Thing happened to me on the way to the Forum' and starred two famous comic characters, *Laureolus et Hardius*. A condemned convict traditionally played the part of Laureolus and he would be slaughtered at the end of the performance! The play had been a great success in Rome, where it had run for 120 nights/convicts.

The party met promptly at sundown outside the amphitheatre, where they all bought bags of rotten fruit and other offensive materials from a street vendor; the contents of which they could hurl at the actors if their performances did not please the audience. Some over-enthusiastic theatregoers had to be relieved of knives, spears, catapults and paving stones by the *ianitore* (bouncers) at the front door.

Sulinus and his friends settled themselves into their seats and bought some refreshments. Amongst the delicacies on offer were lark's tongues, ocelot spleens, dormice in honey and snails fed on raw meat. (To give them body.)

The play began with a blare of trumpets and two characters, wearing grotesque face masks, marched on to the stage from opposite wings. They stopped mid-stage and introduced themselves at the top of their voices.

'I am Laureolus!' shouted the small skinny one.

'And I am Hardius!' yelled the large fat one. 'And don't you forget it!' he added, as he fetched his small companion a sharp slap to the head.

The audience roared with laughter. They always enjoyed the subtle wit and repartee of the theatre!

The plot, such as it was, consisted mainly of slapstick comedy, copious expulsion of bodily gases, crude jokes, huge offensive anatomical models and slanderous comments about senators, consuls and people in authority in general. The main female part was played by a man who was a head and shoulders taller than the rest of the cast and was built like a discus thrower, but no-one seemed to mind.

As was the custom, the performance ended with the slaughter of Laureolus! He was despatched by a huge slave wielding a gigantic club. The slave's whole purpose in the play was to execute the unfortunate actor/criminal!

The play had been a roaring success and received great acclaim from the discerning audience. As a result, there were almost no fatal brawls outside the amphitheatre and the bags of rotten fruit etc. went unused and were sold back to the vendors. The bags would be re-sold at subsequent performances, by which time they would have acquired a little more potency!

'I thought Laureolus et Hardius were hilarious!' said Sulinus, as the group headed towards the *Male Psittacus* tavern.

'I thought the convict who played Laureolus acted the death scene particularly well. It was very realistic' enthused Halitus Malus.

The others just stared at him.

'I thought the chap who played the role of the heroine

had all his muscles in the right place' observed Noelius.

Gayus agreed wholeheartedly.

The *Male Psittacus* was crowded and noisy when Sulinus and his friends walked in. Quite a number of fellow revellers had got there before them and the communal sick buckets at either end of the bar were almost full already.

'Ten goblets of your worst *mulsum*, bar steward!' roared Noelius to the landlord, Caupus.

'Did Noelius just infer that Caupus was born out of wedlock?' said Halitus.

'No. Bar steward is just another name for innkeeper' explained Bilius patiently. He decided against *mulsum* and opted instead for a jar of *Stella Artus*, a popular local beer.

The evening rolled on nicely and the stag party members were feeling decidedly mellow, when a fight broke out in another corner of the inn. Two men were throwing punches at each other, but given their advanced state of inebriation, most of the punches hit mid-air.   However, Sulinus and company went over to enjoy the spectacle.

'That's Ebrius!' exclaimed Brucetus, pointing to the smaller of the two combatants. 'He's the one who built the East Baths, you know.'

'Before they fell down again, you mean' added Noelius dryly.

'My master had to pay a pretty sestertrius to have them rebuilt again' added Halitus. 'No-one knows why they fell down in the first place.'

'Actually, *everyone* knows why they fell down; except this poor sap' whispered Noelius to Brucetus, as he nodded at dim-witted Halitus.

Nasius had gone off to the *latrina* and when he rejoined his companions he was furious.

'Some scoundrels have scrawled graffiti all over the *latrina* walls!' he said. 'They have written; 'ROMANI ITE DOMUM!' *(Romans go home.)* 'How dare they!'

'I know. I saw it earlier. It's not the first time that's happened' said Noelius Covardus. 'At least they got the grammar right this time.'

The rest of the party soon tired of the fisticuffs in the corner and resumed drinking large quantities of *mulsum* at their own end of the bar. Inevitably, the drink took hold in earnest and Marcus and Lucius were the first to end up on the floor; out for the count.

'Those two never could hold their drink' slurred Noelius, as he slid majestically off his seat and landed with a thud face down on the floor beside his two comatose companions.

'I think he's noken his brose!' exclaimed Gayus, before he too joined the trio on the bar room floor.

At this point, as if by magic, the young slave, Belator, appeared in the doorway of the *Male Psittacus*. Sulinus had had the foresight to hire him for the evening, with instructions to come to the inn at midnight and collect the casualties, load them onto his cart and trundle them off to their respective homes.

Those who could still walk staggered off home, singing the latest hits from the *Optimus Viginti* (Top Twenty) and stopping to fill up the occasional *olla urina* (wee pot) at the street corners, from which the by-products of their revelries would eventually be collected to be used in the treatment of cloth!

A day or so later, when everyone had recovered sufficiently, the general opinion was that Sulinus' stag party had been a roaring success...

XII.
Ut Medico Visitabo
(A Visit to the Doctor)

The tale Lucidus had to tell that day was designed to explain what would happen at a doctor's surgery...

The morning after Sulinus' stag party, the waiting room at the local doctor's surgery was filled with the walking wounded from the night before; as well as the usual crop of the halt and the lame.

The doctor was Marcus Medicus, a slender, white haired man with a soft, soothing voice, but with an air of quiet authority about him. Medicus was a Greek by birth who had been brought to Britannia many years before as a slave. He worked hard applying his deep knowledge of medicine and eventually gained his freedom. He had stayed on in Britannia, but was not a great fan of his Roman masters, although he did have a soft spot for the Britons, or at least most of them.

The first patient to be seen that morning was Noelius Covardus, whose normally dignified appearance was somewhat marred by a broken nose, flanked by two black eyes. As Noelius was an important man in Aquae Sulis and a friend of the Overseer, Gaius Tiberinus, he was shown to the head of the queue.

'*Salve*, Noelius Covardus' said the doctor. 'I understand you had a bit of an accident last night. Let me look at the damage. What happened, exactly?'

'I accidently slipped off my seat while dining at the Male Psittacus Inn last night and landed on the floor, but before I could get up again that drunken moron, Halitus Malus, fell on top of me; hence the facial devastation!'

The doctor gently probed Noelius's damaged nose and was greeted with a roar of pain for his troubles!

'Have a care, man!' cried the injured Noelius. 'You're meant to cure, not kill me!'

'Your nose needs to be reset and that cannot be done without some discomfort' said the doctor stiffly, as he reached for a pair of fearsome-looking forceps.

Eventually, after a long struggle and much kicking and swearing, Noelius's nose was reset and bandaged.

'I recommend you apply some raw steak or boiled liver

to your eyes to help reduce the bruising' said the doctor.
'Can I eat it afterwards?' asked Noelius.

'That's up to you.'

'By the way, doctor' said Noelius. 'You perform trepanning, don't you?'

'Yes I do. Why?'

'I wonder if you would consider operating on that moron, Halitus Malus. I would be willing to pay.'

'Why? Does he suffer from an excess of phlegm on the brain?' asked the doctor anxiously.

'I doubt it. In fact, I doubt he has a brain at all! But if you bored a hole in his head, perhaps you could inject some brains into his skull; from an animal, a goat, for instance? Anything would be better than nothing!'

The doctor just glared at Noelius. 'Come back and see me in a week... Next patient!' he shouted to his assistant.

The next patient was a rather green-looking Bilius. He was a wealthy landowner, who had retired some years before and left the running of his estates to his son, Moderatus. Bilius, a good friend of Gaius Calpurnius, was a small, fat bald man. He was popular with his peers, with his friendly and gregarious nature. He had taken early retirement for medical reasons, as he had a problem with his liver. Nowadays the complaint is known as cirrhosis.

'Doctor, I fear there is an imbalance in the four humours within my body' he said. 'Although I have been freely reducing the amount of yellow bile in my body, I feel the humours are still not in balance.'

'When you say you've been reducing your yellow bile, you mean you've been throwing up, don't you?' enquired the doctor.

Er, yes.'

'Perhaps an immodest intake of *mulsum* (wine mixed with honey) may be the cause of your ailment' suggested the doctor. 'I believe you have what is known as *capitis dolor* (a hangover). Go home and deep fry a canary, season it with salt and pepper, then eat it with a little salad. That should cure you.'

'What!' cried Bilius. 'Eat the family pet? Is there no other cure?'

'Well, you could try two raw owl's eggs, mixed with a little wine' said the doctor. 'Also, I suggest that, in future, you line your stomach before you go out drinking. Some roasted sheep's intestines should do the trick; Pliny the Elder swore by this method.

Bilius left looking a lot greener than he had when he had entered.

The next patient was a sorry-looking Ebrius, the

builder. He, like Noelius Covardus, was sporting two black eyes and was missing some front teeth – another casualty of Sulinus' stag night. Ebrius was a regular visitor to the doctor's surgery.

'I wath walking home latht night, doctor, when I thlipped in thum mud and fell on my fathe' he explained.

'I didn't know you had any faith, Ebrius. Are you sure you weren't attacked by a bar room floor?' said the doctor sarcastically.

Ebrius just looked blankly at him.

'Anyway,' the doctor continued, 'apply some raw steak or boiled liver to the swelling around your eyes. That should help reduce the bruising.'

'But I am a poor man, doctor' protested Ebrius. 'I can't afford to buy thteak or liver!'

The doctor was well aware that Ebrius was anything but poor, having acquired a large sum of money for some dodgy building work he had done at the Great Bath some time ago. However, the doctor merely said. 'In that case, I have a cheaper remedy.'

He handed the builder a jar containing two large black leeches. 'Attach one of these *hirudo* under each eye. They will suck out the bad blood.'

Ebrius blanched as he took the jar.

'Can you fixth my teef, doctor?' he enquired.

'It so happens that I have just received a shipment of teeth from Londinium' replied the doctor. 'Freshly extracted from the mouths of executed criminals. That should suit you nicely.'

Ebrius' face took on a strange colour.

'Come back next week and I will insert your new teeth. Ensure you wash your mouth out with salt and water first' said the doctor. 'I have to warn you; it will be a painful process, but at least you will be able to eat solid food again. If you ever do, that is.'

The doctor was well aware that Ebrius' preferred choice of sustenance came in liquid form.

The wise Noelius Covardus had once said that it was just as well that the Roman practice of cremating the dead had ended. 'With the amount of booze old Ebrius puts away, if they ever tried to cremate him half the city would go up in flames!'

And so the day wore on. Along with the genuinely ill, the doctor had to treat a number of patients whose ailments were self-inflicted: the hungover, the battered and bruised, as well as an assortment of cracked ribs and broken bones, mostly caused by falling over after a good night out.

'I wonder if trepanning some of these idiots might not be such a bad idea after all!' he said to his assistant, as they tidied away their instruments at the end of the day.

XIII.
'Quis vistis mea furio?'
('Who stole my clothes?')

Lucidus explained to his discipuli how people prepared themselves when they wished to bathe in the Great Bath. Children were not allowed to use the Bath, so were not familiar with the procedures...

'When people come to bathe in the Great Bath of Aquae Sulis, they first leave their clothing in the apodyterium (changing room), *before going into the tepidarium* (warm room) *where they are covered from head to foot in olive oil prior to entering the caldarium* (hot room). *There they begin to sweat and any dirt, loose skin or loose hair gets caught in the oil. They then return to the tepidarium to be scraped clean by a slave.*

Once clean, they use a plunge pool to get rid of any residual oil; only then can they now bathe in the sacred waters of the Great Bath. However, if the bathers do not pay a slave or attendant to guard their clothes during their absence, there is a risk that the clothes might be stolen. If a theft occurs, the bathers can have a curse written out on a *pewter tablet by the resident scribe. They then throw these tablets into the Sacred Spring and pray that the goddess, Sulis Minerva, will exact some terrible revenge on the thief! This is the story of such a theft'...*

The elderly Marcus Librerius, the resident scribe at the Great Bath, was sitting by the side of the bath one afternoon, putting the finishing touches to a votive offering. The scribe was a gentle, soft-spoken soul of some seventy years. He had been a priest since he was twenty. In appearance he was tall and stooped, almost completely bald, with a long aqualine nose and deep-set friendly eyes. There was an air of wisdom and tranquillity about him.

The votive offering he was preparing was for a grateful worshipper who had, for some time, been suffering from the horrors of chronic constipation. The goddess, Sulis Minerva, had apparently heard the lady's prayers and had alleviated the cause of her distress in rapid and spectacular fashion. So now the lady was making an offering of thanks to the goddess.

As he handed over the pewter offering to the relieved, if pallid, worshipper, Librerius became aware of a large presence looming over his left shoulder.

'Are you t'blueday scraab?!' boomed a loud, raucous voice.

'Pardon?' said Librerius, turning to face the owner of this unpleasant voice.

There stood a large, red-faced man with close-cropped hair and a huge stomach. He was wearing only a short, damp, ill-fitting shift and was oozing ill-temper.

'Ah said, are you t'chap what writes coorses agin them what doos oother people ill?'

'Er, yes. I am the scribe and I do write offerings and curses and other things for those who need them.'

'Weel ah don't give owt for offerings and oother things. Soom booger's knicked all me clobber while ah were bathin' and I want t'booger coorsed!'

'I'm sorry, what happened again?' asked Librerius, struggling to make out what the man was saying.

'Doan't you blueday Sootherners oonderstand plain blueday Latin?!'

'You want me to write out a curse against some person who has stolen your clothes, is that it?'

'Aye, that's reet. Me name's Cantissena and I coom from *Eboracum* (York) in t'North. Ah'm a merchant and ah'm worth a denarius or two, ah can tell thee, boot ah didn't earn me brass joost to have soom cheap booger swipe me duds!'

'Didn't you hire a slave to guard your clothes while you were bathing?' enquired Librerius.

'What! Hand over me brass to soom idle, good-for-noothing slave? Not blueday likely! Any road, ah doan't carry me mooney around wi' me, I keeps it locked oop safe at me lodgings. Ah only brought a *quadrans* (less than one penny) to get into this place and that's blueday robbery an' all! If any of the boogers what works for me took as mooch as a *quadrans* that were mine ah'd feed them to t'blueday lions! Mind, I pays them next to nowt anyway, but they daren'st moan or they'd be out on their blueday ears. Ha, ha!'

Librerius wanted to be done with this unpleasant man as soon as possible, so he took out his list of standard curses and handed it to Cantissena.

'Aye, This one should do t'trick!' he chuckled – "*May the person who stole my clothes drown in his own blood.*" Aye, that'll fix t'booger!'

Librerius wrote out the curse and handed it to Cantissena, who read it through, listing his missing property: one tunic, light brown; one cape, dark red.'

'At least t'booger left me sandals and me belt and me poorse; there's nowt in that any road!' said Cantissena.

'That will be one *dupondius* (about £1.25) please, sir' said Librerius.

'What! More blueday robbery! Any road, I only brought one *quadrans*, as wot I told thee, boot I'll bring your blueday mooney round tomorrow when ah'll expect me clothes to have been found by then; if this *Sulis Minerva* is worth 'er salt!'

He stomped off, still dripping, to throw the curse into the Sacred Spring.

This whole exchange had been witnessed by Belator, the young slave who worked at the Baths. Belator loved the gentle old scribe Librerius and hated the way that the foul-tempered visitor had spoken to him. Belator walked away seething with anger. It was never a good idea to get on the wrong side of him!

The next day, Cantissena returned, and after a prolonged argument with the official who collected the entrance fees, was finally waved through without having to pay another *quadrans*. He marched up to Librerius and threw a *dupondius* at him.

'There's your blood mooney, ye old pirate; now where's me blueday clobber?'

Belator was standing next to the scribe and he spoke up.

'Forgive me, master, but it appears that the goddess has not as yet answered your prayers. She gets many requests and it takes time for her to reply to them all.'

'Well that's no blueday good! Ah'm due to go back oop t'North today and ah can't go home blueday-well dressed like this!'

He was wearing an old, torn tunic that was stretched to bursting over his huge stomach. This was all that could be found at his lodgings.

'Forgive me, master, but I may be able to help' said Belator politely. 'I am the custodian of lost property here at the Baths. We have many items that people lose and as part of our service we wash and, where necessary, repair articles of clothing, then store them awaiting the owners to claim them. However, sometimes they are never claimed, so we put them up for sale at the market at a very cheap price.'

Cantissena's eyes lit up when he heard the word 'cheap'.

'Reet, lad; show us your wares' he said.

Belator led him to the room where all the lost property was stacked and labelled neatly on shelves. After much huffing and puffing, trying on numerous garments that were invariably too small, Cantissena finally settled on a blue tunic and a fine black cape.

'These'll do fine. Near perfect fit; not me choice of

coolers, mind, and the sleeves are a might short. How much for the lot?'

Belator quoted a very reasonable price.

'Ah'll take 'em' said Cantissena, thrusting the money into Belator's hands. 'And here's a *quadrans* for thysen. Doan't say ah'm not generous to a fault! Ah've left me home address wi' that old fool of a scraab and ah'll expect me own duds to be sent on to me as soon as they're found. Well, ah'll be off then. You won't be seein' me in this blueday dump again!'

With that he stomped off into the distance.

Librerius, who had come in and was listening to this exchange turned to the young slave.

'His clothes *won't* be found though, Belator, will they?' Librerius said gently.

'No, master, they won't.'

'Be on your way then, you young scoundrel!' said the old scribe with a little smile.

Lucidus explained to the discipuli how Marcus Librerius knew that Cantissena's clothes would never be found. 'Cantissena was already wearing his own clothes when he left the Baths!

Belator was a crafty young lad with lots of connections in Aquae Sulis and he soon found out who the thief was and where he lived. He went to the thief's house and knocked on the door. A small weasel-faced man opened up.

"I believe you have some property that doesn't belong to you." Belator said, without preamble.

"Clear off, ye young whelp, before I takes me whip

to ye!" snarled the man.

"If you won't talk to me, perhaps you'll talk to my master, Gaius Tiberinus. I'll just go and fetch him" said Belator, turning to walk away.

A magical transformation came over the little thief. Like everyone else in Aquae Sulis, he knew of the powerful overseer, Gaius Tiberinus and of his legendary temper.

"Now just a minute, lad! Just a minute! I may have picked up some things, by mistake, you understand!"

He rushed off inside the house and was back in an instant with Cantissena's tunic and cape. Belator took them and turned away without another word. He took the clothing home to his mother, Clementina, explained what his plans were and asked her to dye them all a different colour for him. He also asked that she make some minor adjustments.

Next morning, when the clothes were dry, Belator took them and added them to his piles of lost property, having first removed any items that might just have fitted Cantissena; thus ensuring that the only items of a suitable size were Cantissena's own clothes!

The old scribe Librerius knew what had transpired and though he normally disapproved of such trickery, he loved young Belator and could think of no-one who more richly deserved to be tricked than the rude and unpleasant Cantissena!

When relating this tale to some friends later that day, Librerius quoted Socrates when he said: "Rudeness is the weak man's imitation of strength".

Cantissena and Belator

XIV.
Peregrinus Altaris Consecrat
(Peregrinus Dedicates an Altar)

Lucidus instructed his discipuli: 'When next you visit the Temple Courtyard, look for a votive altar with the following inscription:
PEREGRINUS SECUNDI FILIUS CIVIS TREVER LOUCETIO MARTI ET NEMETONA VOTUM SOLVIT LIBENS MERITO. *This story relates to that altar.'…*

One afternoon, a large, bearded man, wearing stained, but expensive clothing, came strutting into the Temple Courtyard and looked around him until he spied Belator, the young slave, who was just coming out of the 'Four Seasons' guesthouse.

'You, slave! Kommen Sie hier' he called, waving Belator over.

Belator dutifully approached.

'Mein namen ist Peregrinus, unt I from Trier in

Germania haf come on ze pilgrimage. I an altar vont to build, for my gods dedicating to. This inscription to your scribe take unt a stonemason send for' instructed Peregrinus. 'I vill waiting here be.'

He handed Belator a piece of parchment with some writing on it.

'Yes, master' said the young slave. 'I will return as quickly as possible.'

As he walked away, Belator looked at the inscription. It was not common knowledge that he could read and write. He saw at a glance that Peregrinus' inscription would need some serious editing!

As ordered, Belator took the parchment to Marcus Librerius, the resident scribe, who was sitting in his usual place by the side of the Great Bath, writing out votive offerings for bathers and pilgrims. 'Oh, gods!' moaned the old scribe, as he read Peregrinus' proposed inscription. 'Not another one!'

He had vivid memories of having to try and make sense of what a previous visitor had been saying to him. That visitor had been Cantissena from Eboracum, a man who had upset Belator; much to his cost!

Now Librerius was trying to decipher the pidgin-Latin inscription in front of him.

'I'd better go and speak with this Peregrinus myself. In the meantime, Belator, go and find Brucetus or Sulinus' he said.

Brucetus and Sulinus were local stonemasons and were father and son.

'Guten tag! Ich bin ein Treveran!' began the pilgrim

when Librerius had introduced himself.

'Can we talk in Latin, please?' said Librerius.

'OK. If you vont' said Pergrinus. 'Mein Latin ist sehr gut I t'ink!'

'Can I just clarify what you want inscribed on your altar,' said the scribe. 'It says here:

PEREGRINUS, SON OF THE SECOND TREVERAN, VOWS TO GIVE ONE TO LOUCETIUS MARS AND NEMETONA AND THEY WILL BE FULFILLED, WILLINGLY AND DESERVEDLY!'

Is that what you really want to say?'

'Nein! Nein! Nein!' cried Peregrinus.

'That sounds like an emergency call' thought Librerius.

'Oh, mein Gott! Mein Latin ist not so gut as I t'ink, no?'

'No,' agreed the old scribe.

Librerius took the parchment and his stylus and asked Peregrinus what he *actually* wanted to say.

The large Treveran haltingly, in his pidgin-Latin, explained what he thought he had written. The scribe altered the parchment until it now read:

'PEREGRINUS, SON OF SECUNDUS, A TREVERAN[1], TO LOUCETIUS MARS[2] AND NEMETONA[3,] WILLINGLY AND DESERVEDLY FULFILLED HIS VOW.'

Belator arrived at that moment accompanied by Sulinus, the stonemason.

'Sulinus,' said Librerius 'show this gentleman the range of votive altars you stock and let him choose one. This inscription is to be carved into the altar. Advise Peregrinus how long the task will take and what the cost will be.'

He then dismissed Belator and returned to his seat by the Great Bath.

A few days later, the work was finished and Peregrinus returned to see his altar being erected in the Temple Courtyard. He was accompanied by Belator. After the altar had been blessed by the high priest, Gaius Calpurnius Receptus, Peregrinus turned to Belator and said 'I am vishing a dedication to make at my altar now, slave' he told Belator. 'But the alignment ist not correct. You must moving it be.' Belator put his arms around the heavy altar and tried to move it. It hardly budged. Belator was slightly built and quite small for his 16 years, so this task was almost beyond him.

'Perhaps you could give me a hand, master' he said to Peregrinus.

'Vot! I do not the work of slaves do, *Dummkopf*!' He shouted and he gave Belator a sharp clip round the ear.

It was never a good idea to upset Belator, but he said nothing. He just grabbed the altar and heaved again with a strength fuelled by anger. Eventually, the altar was aligned to Peregrinus' satisfaction. He dismissed the young slave and then went through his devotions.

A week later, Librerius was walking across the Temple Courtyard, heading towards his usual spot by the Great Bath, when he passed the newly-erected altar of Peregrinus. He did a double take and stopped dead in his tracks. Some words had been added to the original inscription!

'Belator!' he shouted to the young lad, who was coming in the opposite direction at that moment. 'Do you know anything about this?' he asked, pointing to the altar.

Belator gazed at the wording on the altar for a moment then said quietly; 'The pilgrim slapped me when I was trying to help him.'

'Nonetheless, this is a consecrated altar and such additions, although you may think them justified, are sacrilegious' the scribe said sternly. 'Have them removed at once.' He carried on his way, leaving a chastened Belator standing by the defaced altar. Despite his stern countenance, Librerius was actually chuckling inside. He loved this mischievous young slave and knew that it was not wise to upset him unnecessarily!

'So, discipuli,' concluded Lucidus. 'When you find the altar of Peregrinus in the Temple Courtyard, look very carefully at the bottom of the inscription. You might just notice that some words were skilfully removed in antiquity. Or again you might not. Legend has it that they once said **"ET CLUNIS CAMELI SUM"** (and I am a camel's backside).'

If the addition had actually existed, it would have been on general display for at least a week before Bladud was obliged to remove it, so visitors to the Temple Courtyard might just have had quite laugh at poor old Peregrinus' expense...!

XV.
Amor et Conjugialis
(Love and Marriage)

For that day's tale, Lucidus explained to his discipuli about the rituals performed at a Roman marriage ceremony…

In a moment of amorous indiscretion, Sulinus, the young stonemason, had got a local lass pregnant and was having to do the honourable thing by her – or else! The young lady's name was Hirsuta, the youngest of nine daughters of a successful businessman; she had just turned fifteen. Hirsuta, as her name suggested, was blessed, or cursed, with more than her fair share of hair! She sported what might be called a 'mono-brow' and it was rumoured that she had to shave her face regularly! Hirsuta was also what might be described as sturdily built. She was less than five feet tall and her detractors claimed that if she had been an inch taller she would have been round!

Despite this, her 'interesting condition' had become apparent at an early stage.

When her father, Felix Obesus, found out that Sulinus had got his youngest daughter pregnant he was apoplectic.

Felix Obesus was a rich trader; a small, fat, humourless, self-important man, who constantly moaned that the gods must hate him as they had, in his opinion, cursed him by giving him nine daughters and no sons. He also wore an ill-fitting wig that he was constantly adjusting. His habitual ill-temper was now fuelled by this latest piece of unwelcome news.

'That Sulinus! That tradesman! That... that labourer!' he raged. 'I'm going to go round to his house and beat him within an inch of his life!'

Hirsuta's mother, Medusa Vehemens, though equally shocked at her daughter's unexpected pregnancy, took a more realistic approach.

'There are several reasons why you shouldn't do that, my dear' she said. 'Firstly, Sulinus is a head and shoulders bigger than you are and is built like a *latrina latericia* (brick ****house). Secondly, in case you'd forgotten, he and his father, Brucetus, are in the middle of doing some major repair work to our villa; they are the best stonemasons in Aquae Sulis and we don't want to upset them. Thirdly, with Sulinus as our son-in-law we would expect a sizeable discount on any future building work. Fourthly, you will be aware that there has been a distinct lack of suitors for the hand of our youngest daughter. The gods have not blessed her with beauty, unlike her sisters. If it were not for the lusty Sulinus, she could still be living under our roof when she's forty!'

Although still angry, Obesus saw the logic in his wife's reasoning and calmed down somewhat.

'A wedding will have to be arranged – and soon!' he said.

'I thought you'd see it my way' said Medusa quietly.

Although she had a fearsome temper and terrified everyone around her, Medusa was an intelligent woman and was more than capable of making her impetuous and none-too-bright spouse come round to her point of view.

Meanwhile, Brucetus, Sulinus' father, when he heard the news, was altogether more sanguine. After all, twenty-five years earlier he had found himself in a similar situation!

'A wedding will have to be arranged – and soon!' he said; unknowingly echoing Obesus' sentiments. 'This could well work to our advantage, Sulinus my son. Old Obesus is very well-connected and an introduction to some of his wealthy friends could bring some very lucrative trade our way! Think of it. You'll be gaining a good wife and I'll be gaining a grandson; someone to carry on the family business in due course.'

'The child *may* be a girl, father' ventured Sulinus.

'Nonsense! There hasn't been a girl born into our side of the family since the time of the Emperor Tiberius, a hundred years ago!

Brucetus did not stop to consider the fact that Hirsuta was one of nine sisters!

And so the wedding was arranged for the first Saturday of *Iunius* (June), after the Haruspex, Marcius Lucius Memor, had been consulted and had established, after reading the liver of a sacrificed goat, that the gods favoured that date.

The day finally arrived and the gods had blessed the occasion with perfect summer weather. In preparation for the marriage ceremony, Hirsuta was dressed up in her bridal clothes; red shoes, a white dress, a red stole and a flame-coloured veil, topped off by a headdress of white flowers. Around her waist she wore a belt which had a knot in it symbolising that her new husband would be 'belted and bound' to her. Only he would untie the knot when they went to their wedding bed.

As was the custom, the marriage was to take place at the home of Hirsuta's parents and the guests began to arrive just after noon. Among the first to arrive were Bilius, Noelius Covardus and Halitus Malus.

As he gazed at the bride, Noelius observed drily, 'Never was a veil more appropriate.'

When everyone was gathered, the ceremony began with the *dextrarum iunctio* (joining of the right hands). The officiating priest, Gaius Calpurnius Receptus, said the wedding prayers and wished the young couple long life, happiness and fertility.

'No problem with the fertility bit' whispered Covardus.

As the ceremony ended, Hirsuta said the words; '*UBI*

TU SULINUS, EGO SULINA' ('you are Sulinus, I am Sulina'), thus confirming her marriage vows by taking her husband's name.

With the ceremony over the bride was able to lift off her veil.

'She *is* rather hirsute; hence the name I suppose' commented Noelius Covardus.

'I wouldn't know about that,' added Halitus Malus. 'But she *does* seem to be rather hairy.'

Not for the first or last time he received a slap from his master, Gaius Tiberinus!

The wedding party then made their way through to the dining room where a sumptuous feast awaited them. As the guests dined, a bevy of scantily-clad dancers glided into the room and began to gyrate wildly amongst the tables, accompanied by the frenzied music of a very accomplished trio of musicians, playing the *tibia*, *tympanum* and *pandura*. (Flute, drum and lute).

As the *mulsum* (wine mixed with honey) began to take effect, several of the male guests lurched to their feet and began to gyrate clumsily with the nubile young dancers. This caused some disgust. It was considered very bad form for Romans to dance with the hired help!

'They remind me of a group of dancing bears' commented Bilius, disdainfully.

'But without a bear's grace or intelligence' added Covardus.

When the dancing ended, the guests threw coins on the floor for the entertainers to scoop up.

Although the dancing had finished, the festivities

carried on unabated and more and more of the party started to lose their inhibitions.

Among the serving staff that day were Belator and his girlfriend, Maria. While diligently serving table, they found time to carefully note who was doing what to whom. The list of indiscretions would be added to their growing dossier of information on the Romans, to be used against them as and when the opportunity arose.

At last, as the sun set, it was time for the final part of the wedding ritual; escorting the newly-married couple to their new home; the house of Sulinus' father, Brucetus.

Three young boys preceded the wedding party with lit torches to guide the way. They were followed by the priest, then the newlyweds and finally the rest of the guests. When they reached Brucetus' home, the young boys threw their torches to the crowd.

Before entering the house, Hirsuta smeared the doorposts with oil then covered them with sheep's wool.

'I've just had them painted too' muttered Brucetus.

And so the wedding day of Sulinus and Hirsuta Sulina ended. The guests staggered their merry way home, while back at Hirsuta's old home, the servants were still clearing up and helping themselves to the banquet leftovers. There were quite a few coins retrieved from the floor where the dancers had missed them.

All in all it was considered a very successful wedding day!

Felix Obesus – Fat Cat
Medusa Vehemens – Poisonous Jellyfish

XVI.
Partus
(Births)

In this tale, Lucidus described to his discipuli the typical rituals of childbirth...

Five months to the day after her wedding, Hirsuta Sulina went into labour. Word quickly spread throughout Aquae Sulis that young Sulinus, the stonemason, was about to become a father.

'They have only been wedded less than half a year and yet a babe is about to be born!' said Halitus Malus, secretary to the Overseer, Gaius Tiberinus. 'I thought it took nine months to produce a baby!'

Halitus was not the sharpest strigil in the box and fully deserved the smack on the head that his master gave him, accompanied by some less-than-complimentary observations about his intellect!

The local *obstetrix* (midwife), Nutricula, was duly summoned to the house of Brucetus, where Sulinus and Hirsuta lived. Nutricula was very fat and jolly and highly experienced in the delivery of babies. Under her large arm she carried a portable *partus sella* (birthing chair), a prerequisite for any obstetrix.

As the midwife laid out her equipment, the assembled families of the young couple made offerings to the goddess Artemis, goddess of labour, and to the goddess Juno, goddess of birth. As was the custom, the female attendants bathed Hirsuta in wine.

'Such a waste of one of life's necessities' said Tiberinus ruefully.

At this point, the men were escorted from the delivery room. This was woman's work.

Nutricula then sprinkled some powdered sow's dung on the young woman's swollen belly to ease the pain.

'I smell halfway between a taverna and a public toilet!' gasped Hirsuta between contractions. The worst was yet to come. The obstetrix poured some mixture into an incense burner and waved it to and fro in front of the young girl's face.

'What in the name of the gods is that!' choked Hirsuta, as a foul stench reached her nostrils.

'Fumigation with the fat of a hyena brings on instant delivery' Nutricula explained.

'But it's foul! It's horrible! I can't breathe! I... Oh! Oh...! OOOH!'

'It never fails' said the obstetrix.' Time to move her to the *partus sella*.' The assembled ladies helped Hirsuta to the birthing chair.

Outside the delivery room, the men, being Romans who did not concern themselves with womanly matters, were consuming heroic quantities of *mulsum* and discussing the merits, or otherwise, of the political classes. This was a favourite topic of influential Roman men. Gaius Tiberinus, being a politician of sorts, was singing the praises of the political system. Noelius Covardus, on the other hand, had a different view.

'My dear Tiberinus,' he drawled, 'I abhor politics and politicians. Politics is the art of preventing people from becoming involved in affairs that concern them.'

'I think you're being a bit unfair, Covardus' countered Tiberinus. 'After all, we need some form of government, otherwise there would be anarchy. Just look at what happened during the civil war before order was restored by the Emperor Vespasian.'

'Well you asked me for my opinion and everyone's entitled to my opinion' sniffed Covardus. 'I think...'

But no-one found out what he thought, for just then the unmistakable cry of a new born baby was heard!

A few moments later, the obstetrix walked into the room carrying a squalling bundle of new life.

'Do I have a son?' cried Sulinus.

'You have a beautiful, healthy baby daughter' said Nutricula.

'Oh' said Sulinus and Brucetus in unison.

'There goes a hundred years of male heirs!' chortled Tiberinus.

'Let's have a look then' said the new father.
He gazed down at his infant daughter. Trying manfully to hide his love and pride, he murmured, 'Girls aren't really so bad after all.'

'You may see the new mother now' said the obstetrix.

Sulinus, Brucetus and the other men shuffled into the delivery room. Sulinus approached the reclining Hirsuta with the intention of placing a kiss on her forehead, but the combined smell of wine, sow's dung and roasted hyena fat stopped him in his tracks!

'What in the name of the gods…!' he spluttered.

'You must kiss your wife. It is the custom' said Tiberinus, from behind the safety of a perfume-soaked napkin. The baby was duly returned to her mother and Sulinus dutifully kissed them both. The presiding priest, Gaius Calpurnius Receptus, presented the new baby with a *bulla*, which he had first blessed.

'May this gift bring you good fortune' he said, as he handed over the bulla. It was a beautiful golden heart on a delicate chain and would stay with the little girl until she became a teenager, when she would be required to surrender it, as she left behind the things of childhood.

Her proud grandfather, Brucetus, came forward with a beautiful wooden crib that he had fashioned with his own hand. Other gifts were brought and placed before the young mother and her new baby.

A celebratory feast had been prepared in the house of

Brucetus and it wasn't long before the hungry gathering descended upon it, once the normal formalities had been observed.

'Have you thought of a name for the child?' Lady Flavia asked Hirsuta, in between mouthfuls of chicken.

'Well, we know that you shouldn't name a baby until it is nine days' old, but we rather like the name of Tintinnabula. It has a ring to it, don't you think?'

'Er, yes' replied Flavia.

'So you have a daughter, eh?' boomed Felix Obesus to Sulinus, throwing his arm round his son-in-law's shoulder. 'Never mind. Look on the bright side. At least you won't have to spend out on an education for her. None of my daughters ever went to school. They can't read or write a word between them and it hasn't done them any harm! Mind you on the other hand, shelling out for wedding dowries can cost an absolute fortune. I should know!'

A rather mellow Brucetus wandered over with a large goblet of mulsum in his hand. 'You know, this is just the first baby' he said, addressing Obesus. 'There will be plenty more and I'll bet they'll all be boys – at least they'd better be!' he said, glaring drunkenly at his son.

Standing a little way off, Gaius Tiberinus and Noelius Covardus were listening to these exchanges. Noelius offered his opinion.

'If the future offspring are as hirsute as their mother they could start their own zoo!'

Before Tiberinus could admonish his friend for his unkind remarks the baby began to wail with renewed vigour.

'Fine pair of lungs' observed Covardus dryly.

'The baby needs feeding' said Nutricula. 'Time for you men to make yourselves scarce.'

The men didn't need a second telling. They had already arranged to repair to the *Male Psittacus* (Sick Parrot) Inn at the earliest opportunity to 'wet the baby's head'. The priest gave his final blessing to the young couple and their baby and then led the charge to the waiting hostelry!

Peace descended over the Brucetus household once again. Sulinus sat quietly with his young family, while in another room; the two grandfathers toasted each other with copious amounts of mulsum and planned the future of their as-yet-unborn grandsons!

XVII.
Mors
(Deaths)

Lucidus told his discipuli about the rituals of death and burial in a Roman town...

One day, the news reached Aquae Sulis that Lady Flavia's mother, Vetula Putrida (Putrid old woman) had just died at the *domus recessus* (retirement home) where she had lived and terrorised everyone for a number of years. When it had become clear that the old woman could no longer cope on her own and would need specialist care (and perhaps padded accommodation), her son-in-law, Gaius Tiberinus, had gone to great lengths to ensure that a suitable care home was found that was at least 25 miles from Aquae Sulis! Flavia, who was blind to her mother's darker side, thought that this was an excessive distance. However, she did have to admit that it was a beautiful home, surrounded by high brambles, a picturesque moat and sentry towers to ensure that unwanted intruders could not get in. It never occurred to her that these were measures designed to prevent the residents from getting out!

The cause of Vetula's death had been lead poisoning. However, when Gaius Calpurnius Receptus, the High Priest, arrived to perform the funerary rites, Tiberinus whispered to him that he believed that she had looked in a mirror before her attendants had had a chance to apply her makeup and the subsequent shock had finished the old girl off! Tiberinus was careful not to share this theory with his wife, Flavia. He had loathed his *socrus* (mother-in-law) from the day he had met her!

Vetula had been universally disliked and feared. Even her powerful son-in-law preferred to give her a wide berth! She was a small, wizened woman with fierce gimlet-eyes that missed nothing. In her need to be noticed, she had recently taken to wearing a bright red wig which only added to her frightening appearance. She had never been known to smile, let alone laugh.

For years, Vetula had been wearing face-whitener made from white lead and although other fashionable ladies had warned her that white lead eventually rotted the skin, and that she should use chalk instead, she dismissed the idea with a snort.

'I'm not going to change my habits at my time of life!' she said scornfully. 'And anyway the gods would never cut short the life of such a devout soul as me!'

But they did.

Funerary preparations had to be made. Accordingly, the old woman's body was brought to the Tiberinus' villa where she would be washed, dressed in her funeral clothes and laid out in the atrium for seven days, as per the custom.

'Seven days!' groaned Tiberinus. 'What a cheery little ornament she'll make! She was none too fragrant to begin with, but seven days…! Oh well, at least it'll keep the flies off the rest of us!'

During the lying in state, Lady Flavia was kept busy organising the mourners list, which included the *praeficae* (professional mourners). She had her slaves running around preparing a sumptuous funeral banquet. Meanwhile, Gaius Tiberinus had the burial site prepared outside the city walls in accordance with the law.

He sent for the stonemasons, Brucetus and Sulinus, and ordered them to prepare a lavish tombstone. He then summoned Belator, the young slave.

'I know you can read and write. Don't deny it' he said, as Belator began to protest. 'So I want you to devise a suitably-worded inscription for Vetula's tombstone. I will instruct you on the general theme. However, as few of us Romans read or write well, we will never know what the inscription *actually* says. If you get my meaning, Belator?'

'Yes, master. I do' replied Belator.

At the end of seven days lying in state, it was time for Vetula Putrida's body to be taken to her final resting place. She was placed in a sumptuous sarcophagus, which had been designed by Brucetus and Sulinus, and was carried by six strong men through the city to the cemetery outside the city walls. The long procession that followed the coffin was made up largely of *praeficae* who would weep and wail for anyone – for a price. In truth, Vetula Putrida had had very few friends in her long lifetime and true mourners would have been very thin on the ground!

Behind the mourners came Vetula's female relatives and behind them the men. There was a marked difference between the anguish of the wailing vanguard and that of the group of men that followed on behind. There, the atmosphere was positively festive!

'I'm curious, old chap' said Noelius Covardus, who was walking by the side of his old friend, Gaius Tiberinus, the 'grieving' son-in-law. 'If you hated the old girl so much, why did you keep her portrait above the fireplace for all those years?'

'It kept the children away from the fire; far better than any fireguard' replied Tiberinus. 'Anyway, I stopped hating her the moment she turned her toes up!'

'I trust you remembered to put Charon's obol in her mouth, otherwise she won't be able to pay her ferry fare across the river Styx to Hades and she may come back to haunt you!' said Covardus.

'Don't worry,' replied Tiberinus, 'I stuffed the old crow's mouth full of coins. You can't be too careful, can you!'

The conversation continued in this disrespectful vein until at last the procession arrived at the burial site. The sarcophagus was duly lowered into its allotted place amid renewed wailing from the *praeficae* and the priest, Gaius Calpurnius Receptus, began to recite the *laudatio funebris* (eulogy), in which he extolled the virtues on the deceased lady at great length.

'Listening to Receptus' speech, it sounds like Putrida wasn't such a bad old stick after all' commented Covardus dryly.

'Do you think so?' replied Tiberinus. 'Have you read the inscription on her tombstone?'

'You know very well that I can't read. That's what we keep scribes for.'

As if on cue, Tiberinus' secretary, Halitus Malus, appeared at his elbow. 'Forgive me, master, but I have serious misgivings about the tombstone inscription' he said.

The secretary, although not the sharpest of men, could nonetheless read and write and he began to read the inscription out loud.

'Stop right there!' hissed Tiberinus. 'I commissioned the wording and I'm happy with it. Understand?'

'Yes, master' gulped the secretary and with that he beat a hasty retreat!

Tiberinus had memorised the wording that Belator had composed and before he lead the procession back to his villa for the funerary banquet he stood in front of the tombstone and mouthed the words silently...

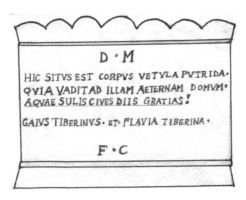

'To the spirit of the departed. In this place lies the body of Vetula Putrida. She goes to her eternal home. The citizens of Aquae Sulis thank the gods! Gaius Tiberinus and Flavia Tiberina set this tombstone up.'

XVIII.
Adventus
(Coming-of-Age)

Lucidus explained the Adventus rituals to his discipuli. He told them that seventeen is the traditional age at which a Roman boy becomes a man and puts aside the things of his childhood in preparation for his new role in life as an adult. At seventeen, the young man surrenders his 'bulla' (a gift – such as a charm bracelet – that was given to him at his birth to protect him until he reaches manhood) and dedicates it to the Lares (household gods), such as Janus, the two-headed god of beginnings and endings (and of doors), and Vesta, the goddess of the hearth. The young man is then enrolled as a full Roman citizen at the Tabularium (town records office).

There was a buzz of excitement around Aquae Sulis one morning in early Martius (March). Maximus Formosus, the eldest son of the High Priest, Gaius Calpurnius Receptus and his wife Trifosa Calpurnia, was about to celebrate his seventeenth birthday.

Maximus was tall and blond with the finely-honed body of an athlete. He had a confident, easy manner and, not surprisingly, was always surrounded by adoring young – and not so young – females. His parents were extremely proud of their handsome son and tended to turn a blind eye to his darker side. His siblings, however, were not so starry-eyed and accordingly were not so enamoured with their eldest brother. He had always been the favourite of their parents and the others; two boys and a girl, named Secundus, Julius and Flavia the Younger (named after her godmother), aged fifteen, thirteen and twelve respectively, had walked in his shadow all of their short lives. They were hard working and serious children, while Maximus was an idle *bon viveur* with an air of arrogance and entitlement about him. Although he knew that he was not over-endowed with intelligence, he felt sure that this would not hinder him in his quest for fame and fortune.

The ceremony began in front of the altar in the Temple Precinct, where the Haruspex, Lucius Marcius Memor, sacrificed a goat and examined its liver. He predicted confidently; 'You will have a long and fruitful life, young Maximus, and will one day become a senator of Rome!'

This prediction was met with loud cheering and clapping from the assembled guests. However, unbeknownst to those present, this was not what the gods had in mind for young Maximus… (See Postscript 1.)

Prior to the Adventus, Gaius Calpurnius Receptus had had a fine *Toga Virilise* (toga of manhood) made for his son and this was now presented to Maximus by his proud godfather, Gaius Tiberinus. Upon receipt of this toga, he laid down his *Toga Praetexta* (toga of childhood) and put on the new toga, again amidst the cheers from the crowd. With this gesture, he had become a grown man and was acknowledged as a full citizen of Rome.

The final part of the ritual, namely the anointing of Maximus with sacred oil and a sumptuous Adventus banquet at which congratulatory speeches would be made, would take place at the home of Gaius Calpurnius Receptus. This was not far from the Temple, so the party made their way there on foot, preceded by a pair of trumpeters whose blaring trumpets warned ordinary plebians to get out of the way of the procession.

At the end of the procession came the servants and slaves who were on hand to attend to the every need of the party. Amongst the servants was young Belator, who was carrying the jar of sacred oil with which Maximus would be anointed.

As he walked along, Belator was joined by Secundus, Julius and Flavia the Younger. The trio was well aware of Belator's legendary intelligence and resourcefulness and they knew that he loathed their arrogant brother, who was only a few months older than Belator himself. Accordingly, they had come prepared with a cunning plan to get one over on the pompous Maximus on this,

his most important day.

Secundus pointed to the jar that Belator was carrying and asked innocently, 'Is that jar well sealed, Belator? We wouldn't want any of the sacred oil to get spilled, would we?'

'No master. But fear not. It is sealed securely with wax and the stamp of your illustrious father, Gaius Calpurnius Receptus and only he may break the seal.'

'Do you mean this wax and seal?' enquired Secundus, handing Belator a small bag.

Without waiting for a reply, he walked off to join the main party.

Belator looked into the bag then called to his girlfriend, Maria, who was walking behind him and whispered something in her ear. Maria then slipped quietly away.

Some time later, the procession duly arrived at the Receptus house and the anointing of Maximus with the sacred oil was solemnly performed, with suitable prayers being offered to the gods.

With that, the feasting could begin. Dancers and musicians poured into the room and the *mulsum* began to flow!

The festivities carried on well into the night and when everyone finally headed for home they agreed that this had been a most successful *Adventus*! However, Maximus' day of glory was to be short-lived...! (See Postscript 2.)

Postscript 1: *Despite the predictions of the Haruspex, Maximus Formosus did not have a long and fruitful life. In fact, he was destined to grow up to be a hedonist and a* *libertine and died of apoplexy in the arms of a concubine at the ripe old age of 24. He probably would have made a good senator!*

Postscript 2: *A few days after the Adventus, Maximus' hair began to fall out in great chunks. Fearing some dreadful disease, his parents rushed him to see the doctor, Marcus Medicus. Marcus duly examined the youth and declared that his hair loss was due to the application of a very strong hair remover! 'Probably a combination of pig fat and bat's blood. Very potent that one' said the doctor.*

The possible cause, it was thought, might be contamination of the sacred oil with which Maximus had been anointed; but the oil had been prepared and blessed by Receptus himself before he sealed the oil jar with his own stamp. At the ceremony the seal had been unbroken, so the oil could not have been interfered with. (Or could it?)

Receptus' seal and wax were, of course, found just where he had left them in his study.

For several weeks thereafter Maximus was obliged to wear a rather ill-fitting wig in order to cover his devastated scalp. Eventually his fine blond hair grew back, but his reputation and self-esteem never fully recovered!

XIX.
Cum Quatuor Temporibus Deversorium (The Four Seasons Guest House)

In this Tale, Lucidus explained to his discipuli the purpose of the Four Seasons Guest House in the Temple Precinct of Aquae Sulis. He also told how the young slave, Belator, had come to a momentous decision...

It was a hot *Dies Veneris* (Friday) afternoon in the month of *Sextilis* (August) and the Temple Precinct was thronged with perspiring citizens and visitors. Belator was busy assisting infirm residents of the Four Seasons Guest House to reach the Sacred Spring, the Immersion Pool and the Great Bath. The Four Seasons Guest House was so named because of the carvings on the front of the building depicting the spirits of Spring, Summer, Autumn and Winter.

The Guest House was reserved for chronically-ill pilgrims who were too weak to travel far unaided, but who, nonetheless, desired to make their offerings at this holy place in the hope that the goddess, Sulis Minerva, would cure them of their ailments. A priest was also at hand to interpret any dreams that sick pilgrims may have had during their stay in the Guest House.

In attendance at the Guest House, as well as the priest, was a doctor who administered various medicines to the sick residents. The medicines included garlic, which was good for the health of the heart; opium, an effective pain-killer (those who were treated with this always came back for more!); cabbage, which was used as a laxative; silphium (also known as laserwort, a type of fennel), which was used to cure coughs, aches and pains and unwashed sheep's wool, which was used to cure sores and boils.

In his medicine chest, the doctor also had arrow extractors, splints, eye ointments and catheters. (Often when one of the latter was produced alarmed patients would exclaim; 'You know where you can stick that!')

Also, in the Guest House, patients could have the afflicted parts of their bodies replicated in various materials and these models would then be thrown into the Sacred Spring in the hope of a cure.

Belator's job there was to help carry those who were too ill to walk. If they required it, he would take them to see his old mentor, Marcus Librerius, the scribe, who would write out their pleas to the goddess Sulis Minerva on pewter tablets and these would also be thrown into the Sacred Spring.

Although Belator had little time for most Romans who had, after all, enslaved him, he was full of compassion for the sick and lame that came to Aquae Sulis in their desperation to seek cures for their afflictions. Many had travelled great distances and had spent what little money they had to come to this place to pray for the goddess's help.

Some of the wealthier supplicants threw jewellery and money onto the Sacred Spring (having first cut a notch out of the coins so that they were no longer legal tender; just in case some unscrupulous persons should retrieve the offerings at a later date and try to spend them!)

As that afternoon wore on and Belator had assisted his last pilgrim of the day, he decided it was time to approach his master, Gaius Tiberinus, the Complex Overseer, and ask to speak to him on a matter of great importance. It was very unusual for a slave to make a direct request to his master, or even to speak before being spoken to, but Belator was a very unusual slave and everyone, including Tiberinus, knew it.

Belator had been planning this moment for most of his young life and now the moment had arrived.

As luck would have it, Tiberinus was in a very expansive mood when he finally arrived in the Temple Precinct, fresh from his swim in the Great Bath. He had also had an invigorating massage and manicure, accompanied by a few glasses of *mulsum*. Belator knew it was now or never.

'Master, may I have a word with you?' he asked politely, as Tiberinus approached him.

The Overseer stopped, rather taken aback, but he recovered quickly. 'How can I help you, young Belator?'

This polite response was a promising start.

'Master I have served you now for eleven years. I have been a true and faithful servant, but now I would like to buy my freedom and that of Maria.'

Tiberinus stared for a moment. He had not expected this.

'You want me to free you?' he repeated.

'Yes, master. Over the years I have saved what money I could and now feel that I have enough to buy our freedom.'

Before Tiberinus could speak, Belator went on. 'I have discussed my idea with the noble Gaius Calpurnius Receptus, Lucius Marcius Memor and Librerius and they have all given me their support.'

'Well, well! Quite the little conspirator aren't you, Belator. And how much exactly, do you think your freedom is worth?'

'I offer you 2000 denarii (*about £20,000 in today's money*) for both our freedoms, master' said Belator quietly.

Tiberinus blanched. At that time the going rate for a decent slave was about 500-600 denarii.

'Where did you get that kind of money?' he demanded.

'As I told you, master,' said the slave, 'I have been putting money by for a number of years. I have invested wisely.'

Tiberinus stared at the young slave standing before him. It was unheard of for a servant to have so much money, unless it had been earned dishonestly. Tiberinus had learned belatedly, however, that Belator could both read and write, thanks to the teaching of the old scribe,

Librerius. He was also aware that Belator had almost certainly read Tiberinus' own correspondence that littered the table in his study; much of which would not bear scrutiny by the legal authorities. Also, Tiberinus had not forgotten that Belator had helped him avoid humiliating disgrace and almost certain imprisonment when, to save himself some money, he had ignored a decree from the Emperor Hadrian. It was Belator's quick thinking and resourcefulness that had saved the day. (See Tale IV). He realised he had little choice but to grant Belator's request.

Tiberinus' dishonesty had cost him dearly in the end and the money Belator was now offering would certainly help him recoup his financial losses. However, despite this, he was angered that he was being out-manoeuvred by one of his slaves. He kept his famous ill-temper under control and said coldly; 'I will agree to free you both on one condition. I have no doubt that you have built up quite a dossier on myself and other Romans in this city. If you destroy all of the records that you have kept, and I mean *all* of them, you may have your freedom upon payment of the agreed sum.'

'Thank you, master!' said Belator. 'Please excuse me.' And he rushed off to tell the good news to Maria.

And so it came to pass that the legal documents were duly drawn up and Belator and his beloved Maria became freedmen and, in time, full Roman citizens.

Lucidus concluded: 'Despite the enormous sum that Belator had paid to Gaius Tiberinus, he was by no means poor. Over eleven years he had, in fact, acquired a small fortune and now had definite plans for the future. You can also be sure that he did not destroy all of his records; just in case…'

XX.
Fabula de Belator
(The Story of Belator)

Devius and Belator

It was the last day of the school term before the summer holidays began. As promised, Lucidus the schoolteacher had been telling his discipuli a Tale of Aquae Sulis' past at the end of each school day. Now it was time for the last story.

'Well, discipuli,' said Lucidus, 'this is the last story of the term and I think it fitting that this story should be about Belator himself. He has featured in many of the tales I have told you over the past few weeks and as you have seen, was a remarkable young man...'

Belator was taken from his home in Germania by Roman soldiers and sold into slavery when he was just five years old. He was brought to the town of Aquae Sulis in the Province of Britannia, where he was bought by Gaius Tiberinus, the Overseer of the Temple and Baths Complex. Here he was put to work helping at the Baths in whatever capacity was required. He was a slave for the next 11 years.

However, it soon became clear that Belator was an extremely intelligent child. One of the first people to notice this was the official scribe at the Great Bath. His name was Marcus Librerius and he took it upon himself to educate this remarkable young slave. However, Librerius felt that it would be best if Belator's ability to read and write was not common knowledge, so this became their secret. The truth was bound to come out someday, but not yet.

As the years passed, Belator developed into a quick-witted and resourceful young man. He was always polite and eager to help. However, if anyone was unjustly rude or cruel to him, or to anyone that he admired, the perpetrator was liable to meet with some serious misfortune! The blame for their misfortune never found its way back to Belator, however! He often used his skills to outwit his mostly semi-literate Roman masters, who had after all, taken away his freedom and accordingly, over the years, he acquired considerable wealth, mostly at their expense.

Although he tried to earn his money honestly, he had no qualms about duping the Romans for whom he worked.

At the age of 16, Belator met and fell in love with a

fellow-slave, a beautiful girl named Maria, who was also 16 years old.

When he judged the time was right, Belator asked his master, Gaius Tiberinus, if could purchase his freedom, and that of Maria's. Tiberinus had no choice but to agree, as he was aware that Belator knew that there were many skeletons in his particular cupboard and a refusal to release the slave might have dire consequences! Also, the price offered was very generous and Tiberinus was very short of money.

Tiberinus took the money and freed the slaves, who immediately got married and applied for Roman citizenship.

However, Tiberinus was a practical man and he felt that he could use the services of this clever young freedman, so he offered him the post of private secretary to himself. The current incumbent was an oaf named Halitus Malus, who had only been hired because, against all the odds, he had learned to read and write (after a fashion), whereas Tiberinus, along with most of his peers, was semi-literate.

However, Belator had politely declined the offer, explaining that he intended to become a scribe and take over the role of official scribe of the Baths when his friend and mentor, Librerius, retired. This would be very soon as the old man's eyesight was failing. Tiberinus felt, in retrospect, that this was probably a better proposition. Having an employee who could out-think and out-manipulate you at will, was probably not such a good idea!

And so, in time, Belator became the new scribe, a post he held with distinction for many years.

As was his habit, he continued to amass a considerable fortune, usually at the expense of the Romans; for, although he was no longer a slave, he had not forgotten his earlier humiliations at their hands!

He and his wife, Maria, bought a fine villa on the south-facing slopes to the north of Aquae Sulis and there they planted vines and began a lucrative wine-producing business. Belator tended his vines when his duties at the Baths permitted.

Eventually, thetime came for Belator himself to retire from public life and he settled down to the life of a rich landowner and wine producer. However, understandably, he never acquired slaves, preferring to pay for his hired help.

Both he and his beloved Maria lived to a great age, surrounded by their children and grandchildren.

'So that is the story of Belator and Maria' Lucidus said to his discipuli, 'and the last story of the school term. In fact, it is the last story I will be telling you, for I am retiring from my post as your schoolmaster as of today.'

This news was greeted with gasps and cries of disbelief. The discipuli pleaded with Lucidus to stay, but in vain.
'I'm touched that you wish me to remain, but my mind is made up. I have been a teacher for over 40 years and I think I've earned my rest. However, I will call in from time to time to check on your progress.'

The old schoolmaster stood up and prepared to dismiss his class for the last time, but before he did he said, 'By the way, I have sold my little house beside the school and am moving to the same villa where Belator and Maria lived and worked the vineyards so many years ago. It is only fitting that I should do so, because you see, dear discipuli, one of Belator and Maria's grandchildren was my own father. Belator and Maria were my great-grandparents! Class dismissed!'

Here end the Little Tales from Aquae Sulis.

Acknowledgements

I dedicate this book to my wife, Pam, and to my children, Robbie and Katie. Thank you for all your patience during the long months I was scribbling away!

In my search for as many facts as possible about the ancient Romans, I have shamelessly plundered ideas from such sources as: Wikipedia, 'Horrible Histories', 'Up Pompeii!', 'Chelmsford 123', 'The Life of Brian', Mary Beard's 'SPQR', the BBC ROME TV series and other accredited publications.

I am also indebted to friends and colleagues who have helped me develop my themes and have given me encouragement when I got discouraged, or when I ran out of ideas (which was frequently!).

I'm especially grateful to Chic Abrahams for proofreading the draft, adding his constructive criticisms (actually, that's an oxymoron) and for helping correct my appalling grammer (sorry, grammar)… See what I mean?

My sincere thanks also go to Douglas Walker, Heather Morris and associates at the Self-Publishing *Partnership* whose professional expertise and patient tolerance knocked my amateurish scribblings into something that I am rather proud of now!

However, without the brilliant illustrations of my friend, Rob Grieve, this book would never have happened.

My most grateful thanks to you, Rob. I owe you bigtime!